The Mystery of Misty Canyon

Nancy saw the silhouette of Renegade running toward the hills. In the moonlight the horse seemed ghostly, a streaking black shape against the bleached grass.

"Come on," she urged General H, and the rangy buckskin responded.

Now Renegade was right ahead of her. The stallion pivoted on his hind legs and took off again at breakneck pace. General H leapt forward, and the night wind rushed at Nancy's face. She squinted at the fleeing stallion.

Suddenly an uneasy sensation came over her. Why did the grass seem to disappear just beyond Renegade?

Then she knew! The edge of the field was a cliff, and Renegade was thundering toward it.

As Nancy watched in horror, the black stallion took a flying leap and disappeared over the edge!

Nancy Drew
Mystery Stories

Available from MINSTREL Books

NANCY DREW MYSTERY STORIES®

86

NANCY DREW®

THE MYSTERY OF MISTY CANYON

CAROLYN KEENE

A MINSTREL® BOOK

PUBLISHED BY POCKET BOOKS

New York   London   Toronto   Sydney   Tokyo

A MINSTREL PAPERBACK *ORIGINAL*

A Minstrel Book published by
POCKET BOOKS, a division of Simon & Schuster Inc.
1230 Avenue of the Americas, New York, NY 10020

ISBN: 0-671-63417-8

First Minstrel Books printing December 1988

10 9 8 7 6 5 4 3 2 1

Contents

1

A Warning

"We're here!" Nancy Drew said from the back-seat of the jeep as it bounced down the rutted lane. Laughing, she held onto her Stetson hat as the jeep roared under an arched sign that read "Calloway Dude Ranch."

"Finally," Bess Marvin groaned. She was clutching the seat next to Nancy. "It seems like we've been on the go for days."

Bess's cousin, George Fayne, sat in the front passenger seat, next to the driver, Mike Mathews. "Come on, Bess, we only left River Heights this morning. It's not even the middle of the after-noon yet!"

"Early this morning seems like an eternity ago," Bess said. But she offered George and Nancy a good-natured smile.

"Welcome to Misty Canyon," Mike said. He was a ranch hand for Calloway Dude Ranch. His hair was straw blond, and Nancy guessed he was about twenty-five.

"*Misty* Canyon?" Nancy repeated. The three girls stared at the Montana ranch land stretching to the surrounding hills. The sun was hot, the air clear and dry.

"Yep. Calloway Ranch is just one of several ranches surrounded by those hills. The whole area is named Misty Canyon because of the steam from the hot springs in the foothills over there." He pointed to a ridge in the distance.

The jeep lurched, and Bess's pale blond hair whipped across her eyes. "I'm not so sure this was such a hot idea," she said.

George glanced over her shoulder and winked at Nancy. "If you think this is bad, Bess, wait till you ride a *real* bronco."

"I've ridden before," Bess replied, shuddering a bit.

"Yes, but not on a Montana-range mustang," George pointed out, her brown eyes gleaming with mischief. Athletic George loved to needle her cousin.

Nancy smothered a smile. "I'm sure not all the horses at the ranch are wild, Bess."

2

"Not all of them." Mike peered over his shoulder and gave Bess an encouraging grin. "We've got horses for everybody—even tenderfeet."

"Good!" Bess said, sending her cousin a triumphant look.

"There must be a few wild mustangs," George commented.

Mike's eyes narrowed as he stared through the grimy windshield. "A few."

In spite of the wind, George managed to open the slick brochure for Calloway Dude Ranch. "What about this one?" she asked, pointing to a picture of a rearing black stallion. "Renegade."

"Renegade?" Bess's blue eyes rounded. She glanced nervously at Nancy.

"No one rides him," Mike said curtly.

"According to this, no one can," George replied. "It says here he was billed as 'the horse no man can ride.'"

"That was in his rodeo days—he's retired."

Nancy was fascinated. "Will we get to see him?" she asked.

Mike's gaze met hers in the rearview mirror. "Take my advice, Nancy. Stay away from Renegade. He's trouble!" He stepped on the gas, and the jeep leapt forward, shimmying on the rutted lane and leaving a plume of dust behind.

Bess giggled. "I think I'll stick with carousel horses."

But Mike's cryptic comments about Renegade

3

intrigued Nancy. As the jeep passed several corrals, she studied the horses, hoping for a glimpse of Renegade. She saw long-legged foals scampering beside mares, dust-covered horses, and red cattle with white faces grazing in the grassy fields. But no sign of a black stallion.

Mike parked the jeep in front of the main house, a two-story structure that had once been painted white. But the paint had peeled and cracked near the windows. The shingled roof had been patched in several spots, and red shutters hung at odd angles from the windows. A covered front porch ran the length of the house and disappeared around one corner. Several of the porch rails sagged.

The girls jumped to the dusty ground. From the yard, Nancy could see the stables, barns, and bunkhouse. All the buildings had once been painted white but now were a weathered gray. The fences leaned, and the whole place had a worn look.

A plump woman with gray hair was waiting near the front door. Nancy wondered if she was Peggy Holgate, the ranch's housekeeper and an old school friend of George's mother. Peggy had invited the three best friends up to the ranch and had promised them room and board in return for a little help in the kitchen.

"Boy, this place sure looks different from the pictures in the brochure," Bess whispered.

"George!" the woman on the porch called, her round face breaking into a smile at the sight of the three girls.

George grabbed her bag and hurried up the steps. "Hi, Peggy," she said. "This is—"

"Bess!" Peggy interrupted. "I've heard a lot about you." Then her gaze swung to Nancy. "And you must be Nancy Drew. Glad to meet you!" She shook Nancy's hand with a firm, warm grasp.

A van roared up and parked near the porch. Like the jeep, it was marked with green letters spelling out "Calloway Ranch" and the silhouette of a rearing black horse.

Just as several people trickled out of the van, a young woman of about twenty with red hair, a smattering of freckles, and a genuine smile pushed open the creaking screen door. "Hi," she said, extending her hand to Nancy as she stepped off the front porch. "I'm Tammy Calloway."

Nancy introduced herself and her friends.

"Glad to see you here." Tammy's green eyes were warm and friendly, but there were tiny lines of strain at the corners of her mouth. "Why don't you go inside while I greet the other guests? You already know Peggy. She's the cook, house-keeper, nurse, and bookkeeper around here. I don't know what I'd do without her!" With another smile, Tammy hurried down the steps to the people gathered around the van.

"I guess you're the right-hand woman around here," Nancy said.

Peggy pressed the wrinkles from her apron. "Oh, Tammy exaggerates! Come on in, and I'll get you settled in your rooms. Then you can come downstairs for some lemonade."

"That sounds like heaven," Bess said.

Nancy reached for her duffel bag, but Peggy said, "Don't worry about your bags. Hank and Mike will take care of them."

The girls followed the plump housekeeper into the ranch house. Inside, the entryway branched off into four different directions. Stairs led up to the bedrooms. Past the staircase, a hall went to the back inside entrance of the kitchen. To the left of the entry was the dining hall with its long tables. Swinging doors opened directly from there into the kitchen. On the right side was the living room, paneled in knotty pine, with worn furniture and braided rugs on the wood floors. Open beams ran the length of the ceiling, and charcoal etchings of covered wagons were mounted on the walls. A river-rock fireplace stood at one end of the room, and its mantel was covered with trophies.

"Did Tammy win all these?" George asked as the friends surveyed the room.

"Every last one of them. She's the best trick rider in the country!" Peggy said proudly. "She learned to ride bareback before she could walk. By the time she was twelve, she was winning at all the local rodeos. She even toured nationally, before she came back here to help out."

"Help out?" Nancy repeated.

Peggy cleared her throat. "Her father needed some help after his, uh, accident," she explained quickly. "Come on, now, let's get you settled." She herded the girls up the wide steps to the second floor.

As she climbed the stairs, Nancy looked at some photographs lining the walls. At the landing, she paused to study a framed black-and-white snapshot. "Is that Tammy's dad?" she asked, pointing at a weathered-looking cowboy.

Peggy's smile faded. "Yes, that's him. He raised Tammy alone. The poor child's mother passed away when she was only five."

"The way Mom tells it, Tammy's like a daughter to you," George said.

Sadness stole over Nancy. She, too, had lost her mother at an early age. Her father, Carson Drew, a lawyer in River Heights, had raised Nancy with the help of Hannah Gruen, the Drews' housekeeper. "Were Tammy and her father close?" she asked Peggy, wondering about Tammy's father's accident.

"They were very close," Peggy said from the top of the stairs.

A worn runner covered the long corridor. Nancy noticed another staircase at the end of the hall.

"That leads directly down to the kitchen," Peggy said, following Nancy's gaze. "And these other doors are rooms for the rest of the guests. This"—she opened a door to the right of the stairs—"is yours." Peggy cracked open a window, and warm air, heavy with the scent of freshly mown hay, wafted inside. "If you ask me, the trouble at this ranch started with that devil horse."

"What devil horse? Renegade?" Nancy asked.

"I don't know why Tammy keeps him around." Peggy pursed her lips together and shouldered open a connecting door. "And this next room," she said, stepping through, "is for the cousins."

George grinned. "Thanks, Peggy."

Nancy's room was furnished with a single bed, a braided rug, a rocking chair, and a bureau. The cousins' room was a little larger and, except for the extra bed, was decorated just as Nancy's was. There were pictures of western landscapes on the walls and stiff muslin curtains on the windows.

"This is great," George decided. "I'll take the bed by the window!" She plopped onto the sagging mattress as if claiming a prize. "That way, I can hear the crickets chirping and the coyotes crying."

"Fine with me," Bess replied.

Peggy opened the door to the hall. "After you've cleaned up, come on down for a snack."

"We will," Nancy promised.

George stuck her head out the window. "If you ask me, this place looks more like a ghost town than a dude ranch."

"It is deserted, isn't it?" Nancy mused. She sat on George's bed and followed her friend's gaze. A few ranch hands were hard at work exercising horses, cleaning saddles and bridles, and repairing fences, but Calloway Dude Ranch was certainly not teeming with activity. "What happened?"

"I don't know the details, but Peggy told Mom that Tammy's father was badly hurt in a riding accident. He couldn't work and let the ranch slide. Tammy gave up her rodeo career and came back to help." George frowned thoughtfully. "Unfortunately, it was too late. The guests began going to the other ranches in the canyon. And then Tammy's father died."

"How sad," Nancy murmured, thinking of her own father and how much he meant to her.

"Did you notice the van that pulled up behind our jeep?" Bess asked. "I'm sure it could hold a lot more people, but only five climbed out, and one was the driver. The brochure said this ranch could accommodate sixty guests. I'll bet there are only about ten of us altogether."

Nancy's brow furrowed. She, too, had thought

9

there would be more people. "Maybe more guests will show up later. There's still a couple of hours before dinner."

"Maybe," George agreed. But she didn't sound convinced.

Just then, Mike Mathews, laden with the girls' luggage, appeared in the doorway. "Here you go."

"I'll take this one," Nancy offered, reaching for a duffel bag with her first name stitched boldly across the canvas. Bess and George claimed their bags, too.

"Looks like you packed for the entire summer," George observed, staring pointedly at Bess's three bags.

"I believe in dressing for every occasion," Bess shot back.

"And then some. This is a *ranch*," George reminded her as Mike left.

Ignoring her cousin, Bess unzipped her bag and pulled out a pink bottle of shampoo. "I don't know about the rest of you, but I'm going to take a long bath."

"And I want to check this place out," Nancy said. She stashed her duffel bag in her room. Then she and George headed downstairs.

In the kitchen, Nancy and George finished tall glasses of lemonade while they asked Peggy questions about the layout of the ranch. Good-naturedly, the housekeeper pointed through the screened window to the stallion barn, bunkhouse, tack room, and foaling shed. Refreshed, the two girls went to explore the ranch and ended up leaning against a fence, watching a ruddy-faced ranch hand train a nervous gray colt.

The colt bucked and reared but finally stood still and accepted the weight of the saddle on its back.

"Want to try and break him?" the ranch hand asked. "Howdy. I'm Will Jennings."

"I think I'll pass," Nancy said with a grin.

"He's a feisty one, that he is," the man said, shoving his hat back and wiping the sweat from his brow.

"Is he related to Renegade?" Nancy asked.

Will's mouth tightened. "No. Not this one."

"Isn't Renegade the most famous horse on the ranch?"

"And the most dangerous," Will said. Then, tipping his hat, he pulled on the lead rope and turned the young horse toward the barn. "I'd better cool this one down. Nice talking to you."

George watched him leave. "No one wants to talk much about Renegade," she observed.

"I've noticed. I wonder why?" Nancy studied the stallion barn, which was off limits to the guests. She noticed that the gate of the paddock was latched securely, to keep visitors from wan-

11

dering into the dusty corral. "I sure would like to get a look at Renegade," she told George as they walked back to the ranch house to change for dinner.

"I knew it," George said with a fond grin. "Now remember, Nancy, the famous amateur detective from River Heights is on vacation. No mysteries, right? That's the deal."

"I remember," Nancy said with a sigh, but Mike and Peggy's attitude about Renegade had sparked her interest.

"I'd better see if Bess fell asleep in the tub," said George, leading the way upstairs.

Nancy chuckled. "She's probably just looking over the ranch hands. I'll meet you in the dining room after I clean up."

After a quick shower, Nancy put on a fresh pair of jeans and a T-shirt. She started downstairs but stopped short on the upper landing.

From below, a man's gruff voice snarled angrily, "You're running out of time, Tammy. You had better face facts!"

Nancy peeked down the stairs. Tammy was blocking the front door. She stood rigidly, her fists planted firmly on her hips, her back to the stairs. There was a man on the porch outside—a short, round man with thin black hair and a flushed face.

"I don't have to take this from you," Tammy said, her trembling voice low.

"You don't have a choice," the man warned. His beady eyes were cold and hard.

Nancy felt a chill dart down her spine as the small man's lips curled. "Up against Vern Landon and Nathaniel Baines, you're nothing, Tammy. Just a has-been rodeo rider with a mortgaged ranch that's falling apart. Not to mention that black devil horse no one can ride!" He turned on his heel and marched across the porch and down the steps.

Tammy's shoulders slumped. She turned, and her eyes met Nancy's.

"I didn't mean to eavesdrop," Nancy apologized as she hurried downstairs. Through the open window, she heard an engine rumble and tires squeal as a long white car roared away from the house.

Tammy shrugged, but her face was pale.

"Are you all right?" asked Nancy. "What was that all about?"

"That was Rob Majors." Tammy's chin quivered, and she swallowed hard. "He's trying to ruin me."

"Why would anyone want to ruin you?" Nancy asked.

"He wants this ranch. It's no secret. Anyone can see that the ranch is in financial trouble," she admitted. "Dad and I took out a big loan a few years ago, when I was making money riding bareback. We bought some new stock, added on

13

to this house, and spent more money than we should have." Tammy sighed. "When Dad had his accident, he couldn't manage this place alone —not even with Hank West, our ranch foreman, helping him. I quit the rodeo and came back to the ranch to give them a hand. That's about the time everything went wrong."

"Why does Rob Majors care?"

"He's a loan officer for the bank. I'm just a few months behind on the loan payments, and he's sure I'll never be able to pay back the money. He's threatening to close the place down."

Nancy studied Tammy's worried face. "He mentioned a couple of other men," she prompted as they walked into the living room.

"Right. Nathaniel Baines. He owns the Circle B, which is a dude ranch nearby and Calloway Ranch's biggest competition."

"Baines?" Nancy repeated thoughtfully. "Is he related to Stella Baines, the rodeo star?"

"He's her father." Tammy glanced around the room at the trophies in glass cases. "When I retired, Stella stepped into my shoes and became the top trick rider and bareback racer."

Nancy remembered the last rodeo she'd seen. Contestants had ridden horses without saddles around a tight ring at breakneck speed.

Tammy touched one of her trophies. "What Rob was saying is that the Calloway Ranch can't compete with the Circle B. So he wants me to sell this place to Vern Landon, a land developer who wants to build condominiums in Misty Canyon."

Nancy glanced through the window at the panorama that stretched to the hills. "It would be a shame to spoil this ranch."

"I won't let it happen!" Tammy said defiantly.

"How are you going to fight back?"

Tammy's green eyes suddenly sparkled. "I've decided to retire from retirement," she said.

"You mean start riding in rodeos again?"

"Why not? There's a huge rodeo planned for the Fourth of July in Boise, Idaho. The biggest ever. The prize money is the best it has ever been. If I can win at Boise, I can make the back payments on the loan. And that's not all—the winner will star in a series of commercials and maybe even get a part in a movie. I could tour nationally and save this place with the money I'd make."

"That would be great!" Nancy said.

A sharp clanging noise rang through the house.

Tammy glanced at her watch. "Supper's on, and we don't want to keep Peggy waiting. I promised her I'd help serve tonight. Besides, I shouldn't be telling you all my troubles."

Nancy followed Tammy into the dining hall, stopping at the entrance to introduce Nancy to the tall, silver-haired ranch foreman, Hank West.

15

He acknowledged Nancy's smile with a curt nod. Nancy saw that George was already seated at a long table.

"What's keeping Bess?" Nancy asked, sliding into the next seat.

"I don't know. While I was in the shower, she told me she was going to take a look around."

"Maybe I'd better go find her," Nancy said. "If she doesn't hurry, she'll miss dinner."

But before Nancy had a chance to stand up, a shriek of terror shattered the still evening air!

2

Renegade

Nancy leapt to her feet and dashed out of the house. As she raced across the yard, she heard another blood-curdling scream. It was coming from the direction of the stallion barn.

It was Bess. She was trapped, flattened against the rough boards of the stallion corral by a huge, muscular black stallion. He reared menacingly. His dark eyes were wild, and his sweaty coat gleamed blue in the glow of the security lamps.

Renegade! Nancy thought fearfully. Her heart leapt to her throat.

"Watch out!" Tammy cried from behind as Nancy vaulted the fence.

The stallion tossed his head, and his hooves slashed through the air only inches away from Bess's face. Nancy waved her arms to distract the angry stallion, and Bess slid toward her friend.

As the horse reared again, Nancy grabbed Bess's arm. "Let's get out of here!" she yelled, dragging Bess to safety. Tammy shut the gate behind them.

"Th-thanks," Bess gasped.

"Are you okay?" Nancy asked.

"I—I think so." Bess shivered as she stared at the horse.

"What's going on?" Hank West demanded, his boots crunching on the gravel as he ran to the paddock. "What were you doing in there?" He turned angrily to Bess. A group of guests had gathered around.

"The gate was open," Bess said. "I-I took a walk. I thought this was a shortcut back to the house."

"The gate was open?" Hank repeated. "You're sure?"

"Yes!"

Nancy stood close to her friend. "Maybe one of the hands forgot to latch it."

"No way! The first rule at a ranch is to close all gates and doors," Hank said, calming down a little, his brows drawn over his eyes in concern. "Are you all right?" he asked Bess.

"I'm fine. Really."

18

"Good." Realizing the guests had followed him and were watching the scene with curious eyes, Hank forced a tired smile. "Come on, folks, the show's over. Let's go back to dinner."

Mike Mathews led the murmuring group away, and Hank's gaze swung back to the three friends. "You, too. All of you," he said quietly as he strode briskly into the paddock to help Tammy with Renegade.

"Before I go back, I'd like to talk to Tammy," Nancy whispered to her friends.

"Why?" George asked.

"I've got a funny feeling that the gate was left open on purpose," Nancy said. Something didn't seem right to her. Too many people at the ranch had made cryptic remarks about Renegade. And now the dangerous stallion had almost injured Bess!

"Why would anyone leave the gate open?" George asked.

"That's what I'd like to find out," Nancy replied, watching Bess's color return. "Are you sure you're okay?"

"Nothing that a double cheese and pepperoni pizza wouldn't fix," Bess said with a wavering smile.

George grinned, glad to see that Bess was back to her usual self. "Well, ma'am," she drawled with a wink, "I'm afraid all we've got here is buffalo steak and black coffee."

Bess made a face. "I bet Peggy has something better than that," she said. "Like dinner!"

Nancy smiled. "I knew it! You've already made friends with Peggy."

"Someone had to help in the kitchen while you two were out exploring," Bess said. "Besides, we have to help her later in the week. Remember?"

"How could I forget?" George groaned. "I hate working in the kitchen!"

Nancy's blue eyes twinkled. "This is going to be better than I thought—Bess on a horse and George wearing an apron! Remind me to keep my camera handy."

George chuckled. "That's right. And Nancy Drew with no mystery to solve. This is one for the record books." George and Bess turned toward the house.

"I'll see you later," Nancy said. Waving to her friends, she ignored Hank's suspicious glare and leaned against the fence. She watched in fascination as Tammy deftly snapped a lead rope to the spooked stallion's halter and began walking Renegade in a small circle. The horse snorted and pawed as he tried to yank the rope from Tammy's hands, but she spoke softly to him.

"Your friend could have been seriously hurt," Hank said as he approached Nancy again. "This horse is a killer."

"A killer?" Nancy repeated. "What do you mean?"

Before he could answer, Tammy had led the agitated stallion to the gate. "Renegade never killed anyone," she argued.

The horse neighed. Lather glistened on his inky coat, and his eyes were rimmed with white.

Hank's gaze narrowed on Renegade. "Believe me, his name fits. That horse is wild, nothing but trouble. Stay away from him." Hank's face softened as he turned to Tammy. He took the lead rope from her hands. "I'll take care of this devil. You take care of *her.*" He nodded in Nancy's direction.

Renegade danced nervously, but Hank jerked hard on the lead rope, forcing the horse to follow.

Frowning, Tammy left the paddock and locked the gate. "Is your friend all right?" she asked anxiously.

"Just a little shaken up, I think."

"I don't blame her. Renegade can be terrifying." She offered Nancy a friendly smile. "But he's not a killer. Hank is stretching the truth a little. Hank gets a little gruff, especially when things don't go just right. He's as worried as I am about the ranch. And he's not fond of Renegade."

"Why not?"

"He blames Renegade for Dad's death." Tammy leaned over the top rail of the fence, and her eyes followed the retreating stallion as Hank led him to the stables.

"Why?"

"It's a long story," she said, "but the problem is Renegade's temper. A few years ago, in Renegade's rodeo days, he was billed as the horse no man could ride. The saying was that a man could rent saddle space on Renegade, but soon he'd go flying. My dad offered a lot of money to any cowboy who could stay on Renegade's back for one minute. No one ever won the money." Tammy's face clouded. "One day, Dad tried to ride Renegade. He was thrown and crippled for life."

"I see," Nancy murmured. "Is that when you decided to retire?"

Tammy nodded. "Dad really needed help here, though he wouldn't admit it. Hank persuaded me to return to the ranch. Despite what you may think, Hank has a heart of gold."

Nancy wasn't so sure. "So Hank blames Renegade for the accident."

"Right. But it wasn't really Renegade's fault. Dad should never have attempted to ride him. Some people, like Hank, wanted Renegade destroyed. Dad wouldn't hear of it. He claimed that Renegade would become the most valuable asset of this ranch because the horse was such a tough bronc and would provide good breeding stock. Dad thought Renegade's foals would become great rodeo horses."

"And have they?"

"Oh, yes! Renegade's first foals are three-year-olds and some of the best rodeo stock in the state," Tammy said proudly. "It was Dad's dream to sell Renegade's offspring to pay off the loan on this ranch. Unfortunately, Dad died last year, before his dreams could come true."

"I'm sorry," Nancy whispered.

"So am I. I miss him. And Dad was the one who really understood the ranching business. Thank goodness for Hank West. He was Dad's best friend." Tammy pushed away from the fence and squared her shoulders. "Come on into the stables. I want to show you something."

Nancy followed Tammy inside. Tammy snapped on the light, and several stallions snorted. She called them by name and patted the velvet-soft muzzles that were thrust over the stall doors as she passed. Following Tammy, Nancy also rubbed the horses' noses and looked into their liquid brown eyes.

They stopped at the end stall. Standing on a bed of straw was Renegade, but now he seemed calm, with no trace of fire in his eyes. "Meet Twister," Tammy said proudly, stroking the black stallion's forehead. "This is the horse I plan to ride in the Independence Day Rodeo. Without him, I probably wouldn't have much chance of winning."

"But he looks just like——"

"Renegade. His twin."

"Twin?" Nancy repeated.

23

"It's rare, but it happens. Unlike Renegade, Twister has the temperament of a kitten—until he's in the rodeo ring. Then he does just what I ask him to do and shows his spirit. He's a real contender, aren't you, boy?" Tammy slipped her hand inside the pocket of her jeans jacket and pulled out a small apple, which she offered to the horse. "Most of the time he's a lamb, but he can really get fired up in the competition. It's almost as if he knows what's expected of him."

"How do you tell the horses apart?" Nancy asked. "Just by the difference in their personalities?"

"That's a big part of it," Tammy said with a laugh. "Actually, Twister and Renegade aren't identical. See that tiny white spot on his right front fetlock?"

Nancy peered into the stall and noticed the tiny crescent-shaped mark above the horse's hoof. "Fetlock? You mean the joint between his knee and hoof?"

"Right—on that tuft of hair. Renegade doesn't have any white markings, but Twister has that mark. Also, both horses wear halters with name plates."

"Isn't Twister valuable?" Nancy asked.

"Very—but Renegade's the proven sire. His foals have shown far more promise than Twister's."

Twister took a step toward Nancy and pushed

his head across the rails. Coal black and tall, he was a beautiful animal. Nancy patted him on his sleek neck, and the big stallion nudged his nose into her arm.

Tammy smiled. "He likes you. Come on. We'd better get to dinner." She snapped off the lights.

As they walked across the yard to the house, Nancy asked, "Who do you think left the gate open?"

"I don't know." Tammy shook her head.

"Has it ever happened before?"

"Once or twice," Tammy admitted, "but always because one of the guests forgot to latch it. It was probably just an accident." She shrugged. "Let's go inside. I want to see your friend and apologize for her encounter with Renegade."

"I'm not sure about this," Bess said, eyeing the horses warily. Though the trail horses seemed docile enough, she was still shaken up from her scare the night before.

"Don't worry. They'll find the right horse for you," Nancy said, offering Bess an encouraging smile.

The girls and the rest of the guests were leaning against a fence the next morning as the stable hands led the horses into a large corral.

"You'll each be responsible for your own horse," Mike Mathews said. "So I'm going to show you how to saddle, bridle, and mount your animal. Then we'll take a short ride. Has anyone here ever ridden before?"

Nancy, Bess, and George raised their hands, and they were placed in a group with Dr. Hobart from Boston. His wife and daughter were in another group along with a family from Kansas and Sam and Ellen Anderson, a couple from Chicago.

Mike assigned each guest a saddle and a horse. He handed Nancy the reins to a buckskin gelding named General H. "You lucked out with this one," Mike said. "He's got spunk. He's one of the best horses on the ranch. Tammy said you have a way with horses and insisted you ride the General."

"Good." Nancy patted General H's tawny back. "I'm sure we'll get along just fine."

While Nancy tightened the cinch around the gelding's belly, Mike helped George, Bess, and Dr. Hobart with their mounts. George wound up astride a bay mare named Whirlwind, who side-stepped anxiously. Bess clung to the saddle horn of her palomino mare, Marshmallow, even though the horse was standing patiently in place.

Tall in the saddle of his own horse, Mike led the others along a dusty, well-worn trail. The path wound through thick stands of pine trees and across a shallow, gurgling creek. The horses picked their way along the trail easily, walking steadily and occasionally breaking into a trot.

On the way home, Mike allowed his group to let their horses stretch their legs.

General H leapt forward, his long legs moving effortlessly as Nancy leaned over his shoulders. The wind caught in her reddish blond hair and rushed past her face as General H raced across the field, hurdled the creek, and landed with a thud on the far bank. By the time they reached the barn, General H had outdistanced even Mike's horse, and Nancy felt a flush on her cheeks.

"You're quite a horsewoman," Mike observed as he pulled up behind her.

"It's easy on this one," Nancy said, patting General H's shoulder.

A movement in a nearby corral caught her attention. In the paddock, Renegade was running and bucking, though no one was riding him. Even in broad daylight, the black horse seemed dangerous. "Who do you think left the gate open last night?" Nancy asked.

Mike's smile fell a little. "How would I know?" he asked. "I was at dinner."

"So were all the guests," Nancy pointed out.

"Maybe one of the new stable boys—or your friend," Mike suggested just as George's mount, Whirlwind, slid to a stop.

The spirited little mare danced sideways as George jumped to the ground.

"Where's Bess?" Nancy asked.

George grinned and slapped the dirt from her hands. "I don't know. Whirlwind left Bess and Dr. Hobart in the dust."

Mike shaded his eyes with his hands and stared across the dry field, frowning. "They should have been in sight by now. I'd better go check on the rest of the group. Can you handle cooling your horses?"

"No problem," Nancy replied. "Unless you want us to help you."

"No. Just tell Tammy where I am. I'll be back soon." He climbed into the saddle. Pressing his heels into his horse's ribs, Mike leaned forward. His mount thundered away.

As they walked their horses back to the barn, Nancy asked George, "Who do you think left the gate open last night?"

"Oh, no you don't, Nancy," George said. "You're not dragging me into a mystery. As far as I'm concerned, someone just didn't latch the gate properly. It was no big deal."

"Maybe." But Nancy wasn't convinced. Her mind was still turning over the possible explanations when she noticed a tall young woman with platinum blond hair walking toward them. The woman was wearing jeans, a silver-trimmed western shirt, a red scarf, and a white hat.

"Hi," the young woman called brightly, flashing perfect teeth. "Have you seen Mike? I'm Stella Baines, a friend of his."

Nancy introduced herself and George, then said, "Mike should be back in a few minutes." She allowed General H one small drink of water before she set him free in the pasture reserved for the riding stock. The buckskin took off, kicking up his heels and joining the herd.

Stella's mouth thinned, and she glanced at her watch. "I don't have much time. I promised Dad I'd be home soon to practice." She looked across the fields as if hoping Mike would suddenly appear.

"Are you going to ride in the Independence Day Rodeo?" George asked as she opened the gate for Whirlwind. The bay sprinted across the field to join General H.

"As a matter of fact, I am," Stella said. She beamed as brightly as the silver buckle on her belt, until she saw Tammy walking quickly their way.

"Hi," Tammy called to Stella before turning to Nancy and George. "Where's the rest of the group?"

"Still on their way," Nancy replied, noticing how Stella's smile fell. "Mike went back to make sure there wasn't any trouble."

"I hope not," Tammy said.

"What's this I hear about you entering the rodeo circuit again?" Stella asked.

"I haven't got much choice," Tammy said, gazing anxiously at the horizon. "My first entry will be at the Independence Day Rodeo in Boise." She squinted into the bright afternoon sun. "Maybe I should go after Mike," she said.

Stella glanced at her watch again, then said, "When you see him, let him know I'm looking for him, okay? I've really got to get home!" Without saying goodbye, she turned on her heel and stomped across the lot to her pickup. She wheeled out of the parking lot in a spray of gravel.

"She didn't seem too happy about your coming out of retirement," Nancy observed.

"She probably doesn't like the idea of having to compete with me again. Her father's ranch is only a few miles down the road, and we've been rivals ever since we were kids." Tammy sighed. "Since Mike started working here, Stella's been hanging around a lot."

"Oh, look! Here they come!" George cried.

Turning, Nancy watched as the rest of the group straggled in. Bess was near the end of the group, but her cheeks were rosy and her eyes bright with excitement.

"What happened?" George asked.

"Dr. Hobart's saddle came loose," Bess said as she dismounted and rubbed Marshmallow's pink nose. "We were waiting for him."

"How was the ride?" Nancy asked.

"Wonderful!" Bess exclaimed as she unbuck-led the cinch and removed Marshmallow's saddle. "Perfect, in fact. You know, I might just surprise both of you and become the best horse-woman on this ranch!" She gave Marshmallow a pat, and the little palomino ambled over to join the rest of the herd.

"And the best dressed!" George quipped.

The dinner bell sounded half an hour later than it had the day before. When Nancy took her place at the table, next to George and Bess, she noticed that Tammy's chair was empty. Some of the ranch hands were muttering among themselves, and Nancy heard only bits of the whispered conversation throughout the meal.

"I don't know why she isn't back yet," Hank West said.

"Don't worry," Mike replied. "She can handle herself."

"Too many strange things are happening around here," another hand added, but he clamped his mouth shut when he caught Nancy's inquisitive gaze.

"Something's wrong," Nancy whispered to her friends. "I'm going to check it out."

"You're imagining things," Bess replied. "Tammy's probably finishing some chores."

"Then why isn't she back for dinner? I think I'll help Peggy in the kitchen. Maybe she knows something. Why don't you stay here and see if you can hear anything else."

Nancy headed for the kitchen, where she found Peggy Holgate bustling around the room. "I thought you might need some help."

"I could use a hand," Peggy admitted. She stopped and glanced nervously out the window into the twilight beyond. "It's just not like Tammy to be gone so long."

"Is she in town?" Nancy asked. She began to arrange plates of chocolate cake on a big tray.

"Heavens, no! She took Twister out for exercise a couple of hours ago, and she said she'd be back in time for supper." The cook's face was lined with concern. "I just don't know what to think—" She stopped suddenly. Nancy whirled around in time to see Peggy's face turn white with fear. "Merciful heavens! It's—it's Twister!" Peggy cried.

Nancy's gaze flew to the open window, and her blood ran cold. A riderless black stallion, his bridle jangling, was galloping into the path of an oncoming car!

3

Twister

Her heart pounding, Nancy shoved open the back door and dashed across the yard to the panicked horse. The car screeched to a halt.

Nancy grabbed for the dangling reins. The stallion reared away, just as Hank West caught up with her and snatched the reins that whipped dangerously close to Nancy's head.

"Whoa, boy," he said soothingly. To Nancy, he barked, "Back away!" Twister shied and reared, rolling his eyes wildly.

Mike Mathews sprinted across the yard. "Where's Tammy?" Mike asked, trying to help Hank control Twister.

"I wish I knew," Hank replied.

Nancy turned toward the car, a long white sedan, but before she had time to think, another voice cut through the air.

"Help! Someone come quick!" one of the hands yelled from the doorway of the stables. "Renegade's gone loco!"

Nancy heard the sound of splintering wood and the thrashing of metal-shod hooves. She started for the door, but Hank blocked her path. "Go back with the other guests, Nancy," he said. "This could be dangerous."

Nancy's gaze shifted once again to the white car. Two men had climbed out. She recognized the shorter man as Rob Majors, the banker, but she didn't know the tall, lanky man with him.

"Nancy!" Untying her apron, Peggy Holgate ran across the yard. "Someone's got to go find Tammy," she said, drawing Nancy aside. "It'll be dark soon, and she's never been gone like this! George's mother told me all about you—how you help the police in River Heights. Can you help us figure out where Tammy is?"

"I'll try. Do you have any idea where Tammy might have ridden Twister?"

Peggy shook her head and rubbed her hands anxiously together. "I wish I did. But there are dozens of trails. She could have taken off anywhere."

"Okay, here's what we'll do," Nancy said,

already forming a plan in her mind. "Some of us will ride horses and use flashlights to cover the trails in the woods. The rest can either drive through the fields or check closer to the main ranch, just in case she was thrown nearby and can't walk."

"Oh, dear," Peggy whispered.

Hank strode out of the stables and caught the tail end of Nancy's plan. "No way," he said, eyeing the group that had gathered on the porch. "You're all guests here. Finding Tammy is my job." Worried, he darted an anxious look toward Rob Majors.

"I want to help," Nancy insisted.

"Listen to me!" Hank snapped. "I'm not about to let our guests go traipsing around in those mountains!" He waved toward the wooded foothills. "We could lose the whole lot of you. The boys and I will handle it!" He tried to get the attention of the group. "Everyone go inside. There's checkers and cards in the den, and Mike here will serenade you on the guitar and harmonica." Most of the guests appeared less than enthusiastic, but they allowed Mike to shepherd them back into the ranch house. Nancy didn't go.

"I really think I could help," Nancy told Hank as Rob Majors and the other man approached. The lanky man with Rob had harsh features, silver hair, and an air of quiet authority.

"I nearly hit that horse!" Rob Majors was obviously shaken. His eyes on Hank, he demanded, "Where's Tammy?"

"She's not here right now."

The banker's face fell. "But Vern and I were supposed to meet her tonight—"

Nancy glanced at the tall, hard-looking man. So this was Vern Landon, the land developer who wanted Tammy's ranch.

"I called her this afternoon to remind her," Rob insisted.

Hank leaned against the porch rail. "I guess you'll have to reschedule," he said, his gaze sliding from the short man to the tall one. "Tammy's missing."

"Missing?" Rob repeated angrily. "You expect me to believe that?"

"Believe what you want," Hank drawled.

"She's probably just trying to dodge us," Rob said testily.

"Why would she do that?" Nancy asked.

Rob Majors ignored her and glared at Hank. "You know as well as I do that she won't face the fact that this ranch is dying. Mr. Landon has a reasonable offer for her."

"I guess he'll have to take it up with her later," Hank suggested. "But don't plan on giving her any trouble, because if you do, you'll have to answer to me!"

Vern Landon grimaced and fiddled with the

strings of his western tie. "Let's get out of here," he muttered.

"Good idea," Hank said before Rob could answer. Turning to Nancy, Hank added, "Maybe you should go into the ranch house and join your friends. I'll find Tammy." He strode toward the bunkhouse.

Nancy had no intention of waiting around the ranch while Tammy was somewhere in the woods alone. She walked up the steps of the front porch but glanced over her shoulder at the two men.

Landon and Majors had climbed back into the car. The passenger window was open, and Nancy could hear part of their conversation. Vern Landon's gravelly voice was harsh and furious. "Don't worry, Rob. Tammy Calloway can't duck me forever. She's only prolonging the agony. One way or another, I intend to get this ranch away from her. And no one is going to stop me!"

Convinced that Tammy was in serious trouble, Nancy hurried inside the house and found George and Bess sitting in the dining room with Peggy Holgate.

"Is Tammy back yet?" Bess asked hopefully.

Nancy shook her head. "Not yet. But I don't think we should wait any longer."

"Neither do I!" Peggy agreed. "I'll round up those guests who want to help."

"Count me in," George volunteered.

"Me, too," Bess said.

The swinging doors banged open, and Hank West strode over to the table. His eyes were shadowed with worry. "The boys and I are going out looking for Tammy," he said to Peggy. "I want everyone else to stay in the house, and that includes *them*." He indicated Nancy, Bess, and George. "I don't want any of the guests getting involved. They could get hurt."

"But Nancy Drew is a famous detective—"

"We don't need any guests playing detective," Hank replied angrily. "Maybe a tracker, but no girl private eyes." His stern gaze rested on Nancy for a minute. "Jimmy and a few of the boys will search the southern hills. Mike and I will drive the fields. We'll be back in a couple of hours." He frowned pointedly at Nancy. "You stay put. If you want to help, stick close to the phone in case Tammy calls, and keep the other guests entertained." With that, he stomped off. A few minutes later, Nancy heard the sound of a truck's engine sparking to life.

She didn't like disobeying orders—but in this case she was sure she would be more helpful outside tracking Tammy than sitting and worrying in the ranch house. Glancing at George, she read disappointment in her friend's face.

"You're just going to hang around here?" George asked.

Nancy shook her head. "I thought I'd saddle up General H and look in the hills."

"I knew it!" said George with a grin.

Nancy smiled back. Then she added, "But Hank's right. Someone should stay by the phone and keep the rest of the guests from worrying."

"I can handle that," Bess said.

"And I'll help," Peggy offered. "I've got a few old trail maps." She rummaged in a drawer near the pantry. "Here they are!" Spreading the maps on the table, she pointed out Tammy's favorite routes. "I can't be certain which one she took, but she was partial to the hot springs."

"We saw that trail earlier today on our ride," Nancy said, her thoughts running ahead as she studied the wrinkled old maps. Where was the most likely place Tammy would have taken Twister?

"Looks like I've got the easy job," Bess said with a smile.

"Not really. If Tammy does return, I want you to send up flares or have one of the hands shoot his rifle into the air—just so George and I know she's safe."

"There are flares in the tack room," Peggy said, "and believe it or not, I can handle a rifle."

Nancy grinned. "Good. We'll start on the trail to the hot springs. See you later," she called over her shoulder. She and George grabbed their jackets and hurried out the front door.

Outside, pale light from a full moon illuminated the connecting pastures in eerie shades of blue and gray. In the distance, the red glow of taillights from Hank West's truck bounced across the southern fields.

Within minutes, the girls caught and saddled the horses they'd ridden earlier in the day. George swung a leg over Whirlwind's back. "Hank West said Jimmy Robbins and some of the hands are searching the hills to the south," she said.

"Our trail is north."

"Maybe we can beat them at their own game," George said with a knowing grin.

"At least we'll cut the search area in half." Nancy grabbed General H's reins and swung into the saddle. "The way I figure it, Tammy didn't intend to be gone long, because it was already late when she left. She just wanted to stretch Twister's legs. Let's go!" She leaned forward, and General H sprang ahead. Whirlwind whinnied and followed close behind.

The horses sprinted across the same field they'd crossed earlier in the day, then trotted eagerly to the edge of the dark, forested hills.

"Are you sure this is the right way?" George asked after a while, glancing through the trees. "It's sure creepier in here at night!"

Nancy couldn't help but agree as she swept the beam of the flashlight in a broad arc through the ghostly-looking pines. "It's the same trail we were on earlier."

George urged her mount forward, and Whirlwind caught up with General H. "I hope we find her soon."

Nancy swung the light to the right. "That makes two of us." She told George about the conversation she'd overheard between Vern Landon and Rob Majors. "It's funny," she thought aloud.

"What is?" George asked.

"Ever since we got here, odd things have been happening. Someone left the gate to Renegade's paddock open last night, now Tammy's missing, and Vern Landon is making threats. Everyone, including Hank West and Mike Mathews, acts as if they've got something to hide."

"I think your imagination's working overtime again!"

Nancy felt General H tense. "What is it, boy?" she asked, the hairs on the back of her neck rising. General H sidestepped nervously.

Nancy heard a loud hoot, then the flapping of huge wings as an owl swooped down from overhead. General H shied, snorting nervously and half rearing. Nancy scrambled for the reins with one hand, trying to keep her hold on the flashlight with the other. The beam swung wildly across the trail ahead.

41

"Hey, what's going on?" George said as Whirlwind tried to bolt.

"I don't know." Suddenly, Nancy gasped. There was a figure on the path ahead—a figure that was dark and crumpled. A figure that didn't move!

4

Vanished!

Instantly, Nancy jumped off her horse and knelt beside the inert figure. She checked for a pulse, then turned and called, "It's Tammy!"

George hopped to the ground. "Is she—?"

"She's alive!" Nancy cried, relieved at the strong pulse beneath her fingers. "Tammy, it's Nancy. Can you hear me?"

"Oohh," Tammy moaned. Her eyes fluttered open, only to close again. "Nancy?" she whispered through dry lips. "What—what happened?" Squinting one eye open, Tammy tried to sit up, then pressed a palm to her forehead.

"Don't move," Nancy ordered. "You may have broken something."

"No, I don't think so," Tammy whispered, her face ghostly pale in the flashlight beam. "I feel like I've been run over by a truck. Every muscle in my body aches, and my head—" She winced.

"You probably hit it on something," Nancy said. "Maybe you should lie back down. I'll get Dr. Hobart."

"No way," Tammy protested. She seemed to notice the darkness for the first time. "It looks like I've been here long enough as it is. Just help me to my feet." She slung one arm around Nancy's shoulders and the other around George's. Slowly, Tammy stood on wobbly legs.

"Are you sure you can ride?" Nancy asked.

"Positive," Tammy insisted, though her voice shook a little. "When you grow up riding rodeo horses, you get used to spills."

Nancy and George helped Tammy climb onto Whirlwind's back. The two friends doubled up on General H. With the flashlight beam shining ahead, they rode slowly down the foothills and through the huge field Nancy and George had recently crossed.

"Where's Twister?" Tammy asked worriedly.

"Back at the ranch. He was pretty wild when he came back. Hank and Mike had trouble getting him into his stall."

"That's odd," Tammy murmured.

"Whatever's gotten into Twister has spread to

Renegade," George added. "He was kicking up a storm in the stables."

"Great," Tammy said with a sigh. She gazed thoughtfully into the darkness. "The horses have been acting so strange lately. I just don't understand it."

"What do you mean?" Nancy asked.

"Things have been happening—things I can't explain," she answered. "Last week, Twister wouldn't eat. He seemed more nervous than usual. Yesterday, someone left the gate open, and now this. . . ." Her voice trailed off.

"Do you remember what happened while you were riding Twister?" Nancy asked.

"It's pretty fuzzy," Tammy said. "I remember saddling Twister and riding him across here. But he was nervous and out of sorts. I thought he just needed to loosen up, so I let him have his head, and he took me for the ride of my life across this field. Then, once we were in the trees, he got restless and skittish. He must have heard something, because just under a stand of pine, he started bucking and kicking. Then he reared, and I hit the back of my head on something, probably a branch. Anyway, the next thing I knew, there you were." She glanced over at the two friends. "Thanks for finding me."

"Glad to help out," Nancy replied.

The ranch was ablaze with lights. Voices carried through the darkness. One of the hands spotted Tammy and fired a flare into the air. As Nancy, George, and Tammy rode into the yard, they were greeted with shouts of delight.

A few minutes later, just as Tammy was slowly dismounting, Hank drove up, then hurried from his truck. At the sight of Tammy, his weathered face split into a relieved grin. "You had us all so scared we couldn't think straight!" he chided, hugging her. "Are you all right?"

"I—I think so," Tammy replied.

Hank turned to Nancy. "Maybe I was wrong about you, Nancy Drew," he allowed. "But the next time, when I give an order, I expect it to be followed. What you did was brave but dangerous."

The kitchen door burst open. Clutching her apron, Peggy dashed down the porch steps and across the yard. "Thank heavens they found you!" She folded Tammy into her arms, then held her at arm's length to survey her white face. "You march right up to your room, and I'll send up that doctor. You nearly scared the life out of me!"

Nancy and George unsaddled their horses, cleaned up, and joined Bess in the living room. Sitting on a worn leather couch covered with an Indian blanket, Bess was just finishing a game of checkers with Sam Anderson, one of the guests.

"Did you find her?" Bess asked, looking up eagerly.

"Tammy's already upstairs. She'll be okay," Nancy said.

"Thank goodness! I knew you'd find her!" Bess jumped the last three of Sam's playing pieces and got up to join her friends.

Grinning, Sam teased, "You must've cheated."

His wife, Ellen, shook her head, and her dark hair gleamed. "Nope. I watched. She won fair and square."

"How about a rematch?" Sam asked.

"Maybe later." Bess flashed a dimpled grin.

"I don't suppose you mentioned to Sam that you were the sixth-grade champion checkers player at River Heights Elementary?" George asked dryly.

"He didn't ask," Bess said.

George groaned.

Bess started for the kitchen. "Peggy has some hot chocolate for you," she said, motioning for her friends to follow. "Come on. I want to hear all about how you found Tammy."

While sipping cocoa, Nancy and George filled Bess in on the details. "What do you suppose spooked Twister?" Bess asked when she heard about the accident.

"I don't know." Nancy swirled cocoa in her cup.

"Nancy's starting to smell a mystery," George said.

47

"I knew it!" Bess said. "I saw that gleam in your eye last night, Nancy Drew!"

Nancy shrugged. "You have to admit, some pretty odd things have happened lately. Even Tammy thinks so." She told Bess about the conversation between Rob Majors and Vern Landon.

After finishing their cocoa, the friends headed upstairs. Bess and George headed for their room, and Nancy knocked softly on Tammy's door. It swung open. Tammy was in her nightgown and sitting up in bed.

"What did the doctor say?" Nancy asked as Tammy waved her inside the pine-paneled room.

"Nothing good. He wants me to take it easy for a few days." Tammy frowned. "That's impossible! I've got to get in shape for the rodeo. It's my only chance to save the ranch!"

"I'm sure you'll be on your feet in no time and can start training again," Nancy said encouragingly as she shut the door behind her.

Tammy grinned a bit. "I hope you're right."

"Sure I am. From what you tell me about Twister, the two of you are unbeatable!"

Tammy laughed. "Don't let Stella Baines hear you say that!"

A board creaked in the hallway outside, and Nancy looked over her shoulder toward the door. No one knocked. Nancy turned to Tammy again, then heard the sound of a boot scuffing the floor outside the bedroom door. Was someone trying to eavesdrop on their conversation?

"Nancy?" Tammy said as Nancy silently crossed the room and put a finger to her lips.

She yanked hard on the door. It swung open. But the hallway was empty.

"What's going on?" Tammy asked.

That's what I'd like to know, Nancy thought, but she didn't tell her worries to Tammy. "Nothing, I guess," Nancy said, her gaze sweeping in both directions down the hall. She could hear noises from the other rooms in the upper story as guests moved about. "Are all the rooms in this wing occupied?"

Tammy thought for a minute. "Most," she said. "But I think the room across from yours is vacant. Why?"

"I thought I heard someone out there," Nancy said, then smiled. "Just a little while ago, George and Bess accused me of trying to stir up a mystery."

Tammy met Nancy's gaze boldly. "Peggy told me all about you. While you and George were out looking for me, Bess explained to Peggy that you've helped your father and the police with tons of cases."

"That might be a slight exaggeration," Nancy said.

"Not to hear Bess tell it. Anyway, I was hoping that you'd help me."

49

Nancy sat on the corner of the old four-poster bed. "How?"

"I'd just like you to check out all the weird things that have been happening around here lately," Tammy said. "I'd do it myself, but as soon as I'm out of bed, I've got to start practicing again."

"I'll be glad to help," Nancy offered, her pulse racing at the thought of a mystery, no matter how small.

"It's probably all just coincidence," Tammy continued. "But I get the feeling that something or somebody is trying to sabotage the ranch. Crazy, huh?"

"I don't think so," Nancy answered, thinking that everything seemed strange to her, too. "Now, why don't you tell me about Twister? Do you have any idea why he's acting up?"

The floorboards creaked again. There was a sharp knock, and the door banged open. Nancy turned swiftly to find Hank West standing in the doorway. His face was smeared with mud, his clothes were torn, and his eyes blazed furiously.

"I'll tell you why he's acting up, Nancy," he said, all of his friendliness gone. "Because he's a devil, just like his brother! Those two demons are tearing the stables apart, and Twister is as bad as his brother!"

Before Tammy could respond, Hank had turned and was gone.

Nancy followed Hank out of the room.

"Nancy," George called through the open door of her room. "What's going on?"

Nancy stopped for a moment and watched Hank disappear down the back stairs. "Hank said both Renegade and Twister were acting up. My guess is that one or both of them are tearing the stables apart."

"What can I do to help?" George asked.

"Help by staying with Tammy," Nancy said, taking off after Hank again.

Outside, the yard was a madhouse. Ranch hands were running from the bunkhouse and stables, across the yard, and into the stallion barn.

Nancy sprinted across the yard just as Hank West climbed into a pickup and, with the tires spraying gravel, gunned away through an open gate to the pasture beyond.

"What's happening?" Nancy asked.

Mike Mathews stood near the fence, one sleeve rolled up to display an ugly purple bruise. "Renegade's escaped," he said tersely as he rubbed his arm. "He nailed me with one of his hooves, then kicked open his stall. Now he's taking off for the hills!"

Jimmy Robbins and another young hand jumped into the jeep and took off after Hank. Nancy didn't wait. She ran into the tack room, grabbed a bridle, and vaulted a nearby fence.

The trail horses stood restlessly near a stand of oak, their ears pricked toward the chaotic noise.

General H's tawny coat was easy to spot in the moonlight. "Come on, boy," Nancy said. The big buckskin nickered as Nancy strapped the bridle to his head. She tied him to the fence, then dashed back to the tack room for a saddle and flashlight. When the cinch was tightened, she whispered, "Let's hope we can catch them."

Climbing onto the horse's broad back, Nancy urged him across the field that Renegade had raced across. Though the black stallion had a good head start, Nancy knew that she and General H should be able to cut him off at an angle.

She could see the headlights of the jeep and Hank's pickup illuminating the darkness.

Nancy's gaze swept the fields. She saw the silhouette of Renegade running toward the hills. In the moonlight, the horse seemed ghostly, a streaking black shape against the bleached grass.

"Come on, come on," she urged General H, and the rangy buckskin responded.

Fortunately, the gate was open. General H galloped through after the shadowy horse and the winking taillights.

Renegade tore into the trees at full speed. Hank West's truck screeched to a stop at the edge of the woods. Jimmy Robbins also slammed on his brakes.

Nancy heard the sound of other horses behind

her, as well as Hank's rough voice. "Hey—
Nancy! It's dangerous up there! There's a creek
and ravine. Hey! Don't you go—"

But she didn't listen. Bending low over General
H's shoulders, she leaned forward and pressed
her knees into his sides. He disappeared into the
trees, and the night closed in around them.

Nancy searched the darkness, training her
flashlight ahead. But every time she caught a
glimpse of Renegade, he disappeared around a
bend in the trail, leaving behind a plume of dust
that clogged her throat.

Her own horse was tiring, and Nancy almost
turned around. This was the third time General
H had gamely raced for her in one day. She
patted his sweaty neck. Ahead the trees parted.
Once again, she and her horse were on rolling
hills of dry grass.

The moon cast pale shadows over the land, and
then Nancy caught a clear sight of Renegade. He
was right ahead of her. The stallion pivoted on his
hind legs and took off again at a breakneck pace.

General H leapt forward, but not before
Nancy's breath caught in her throat. In the
moonlight, she thought she saw a rider on Renegade's gleaming back! There was something—a
sparkle of something silvery in the moonlight—
then nothing.

Was her mind playing tricks on her? A rider on
Renegade? But that was impossible!

The night wind rushed at Nancy's face. She squinted at the fleeing stallion, trying to make out the shape of a rider hunched over his powerful shoulders.

But Renegade was galloping all out. General H stumbled. Nancy pitched forward, only to grab the saddle horn just as General H caught himself. Nancy tugged on the reins, slowing him.

Renegade streaked across the hill. Nancy squinted hard. *Was* there a rider on the black stallion's back?

She was so caught up in trying to see a rider, she didn't notice that the field Renegade was running across gave way to blackness. Suddenly, an uneasy sensation came over her. Why did the grass seem to disappear just beyond Renegade?

Then she knew! The edge of the field was a cliff, and Renegade was thundering toward it!

Heart in her throat, Nancy kicked General H, and he leapt forward. "Stop!" she cried to the fleeing stallion, but her words were lost on the wind.

Renegade skidded as he reached the ravine, but he was going too fast and couldn't stop.

Nancy watched in horror as he took a flying leap and disappeared over the edge!

5

Bad Blood

Nancy urged General H to the edge of the ravine and stopped. Dreading what she might see, she stared over the rim, her eyes searching the darkness.

With relief, she saw that the cliff wasn't too high. But the drop was sheer, and Renegade could have injured himself by jumping to the ravine floor, where a creek wound like a silver snake.

Nancy swung to the ground and tied General H to a nearby bush. Switching on her flashlight, she scrambled down the steep embankment. She followed the course of the stream, searching for some sign of Renegade. But she could see no trace of the black stallion.

She listened but couldn't hear the sound of hoofbeats, either. Had Renegade splashed his way up or down the stream? Or had someone ridden him to the opposite bank to hide in the surrounding brush? She swept the pale beam of her flashlight along the far bank but saw nothing.

Disappointed, Nancy crawled up the bank and climbed onto General H. Pondering all the strange events at the ranch, she slowly walked her mount across the field and through the woods.

Hank West was right where she'd left him at the edge of the forest. Mike Mathews, on his horse, had joined him.

"There you are!" Mike said, obviously relieved. "I tried to follow you but couldn't catch up. Where's Renegade?"

"I lost him," Nancy admitted. She explained how Renegade had jumped the embankment and disappeared into the night.

"Well, we may as well give up for now," Hank decided. "Not much more we can do until daylight." He cast Nancy a wary glance. "Next time," he suggested, "leave the horses to us."

"Tammy asked me to help," she explained.

Hank grumbled about know-it-all tenderfeet as he climbed into the cab of his truck. Nancy rode back to the ranch along with Mike.

Nancy asked Mike, "Were you actually in the stables with Renegade when he escaped?"

"No."

"But I thought—"

Mike cut her off. "I said that he kicked me. I went into the washroom to check the damage. While I was there, he kicked his way out and took off."

"So you didn't actually see him leave?"

Mike eyed her curiously. "Not really."

"Did anyone see him in the yard?" she asked. "As he ran under the security lamps, did anyone get a good look at him?"

"I don't know," Mike said with a shrug. "What're you getting at?"

"I just wondered if it was possible that someone may have ridden him from the stables."

"Renegade?" Mike laughed scornfully. "No way! Don't you remember? He's the horse no man can ride!"

Nancy kept her thoughts to herself on the way back to the ranch.

"I'll take care of the General," Mike offered as they rode into the yard together.

"No need," Nancy said quickly. "He's my responsibility. I'll walk and brush him, then check his feed."

Mike shrugged. "Have it your way," he added. "But remember what Hank said." Then, hearing the sounds of a horse kicking wildly, he turned toward the stallion barn. "Now what?" he asked.

Though he didn't ask for her help, Nancy followed Mike into the stallion barn. The old building was ablaze with light, and several hands were attempting to calm down Twister.

"What happened to him?" Mike demanded.

"Beats me," one rangy-looking hand said. "I guess Hank's theory is true. Bad blood."

Nancy wasn't so sure.

"Whoa—slow down," Mike murmured softly to the horse, walking slowly into the stall.

"He's been in a frenzy all night," the hand said.

"I just don't understand why he's been acting up," Mike said. The stallion pawed the straw in his box.

"Maybe he ate something he shouldn't have," Nancy suggested.

Three pairs of eyes glanced disdainfully at her. "That's impossible. These horses all eat the best feed money can buy," one hand said. "And we feed the horses ourselves."

"That may be true, but if Twister's temperament has changed, there has to be a reason for it."

"Yeah—like he was born bad!" one stable boy declared.

"Horses don't change overnight, do they?" Nancy asked.

58

"Not usually," Mike admitted as he quieted the nervous stallion. "But it's been known to happen."

"Maybe someone put something in his feed," Nancy persisted.

"No one at this ranch would harm any of the horses," Mike said, then clamped his mouth shut. Twister kicked again, and Nancy noted the white crescent mark on his fetlock.

"He's acting just like Renegade," one of the hands said.

"Not quite," replied another. "This is calm for Renegade."

"Listen, I have work to do," Mike said, tight-lipped. "Didn't Hank tell you to leave the horses to us, Nancy?"

More determined than ever to find out what was going on, Nancy marched toward Renegade's stall. It was empty. The straw was kicked around, and one of the slats of the stall gate was smashed. Black horse hair and several grooved impressions of horseshoes showed on the splintered wood. But the box itself seemed normal: straw, a feed bag, a water bucket, and a half-eaten apple.

Nothing out of the ordinary. Still, Nancy's mind was working overtime as she hurried to see to General H.

The moon had settled low in the sky, and the wind felt cool against her face. Why, she wondered, would a horse "go bad"? Could Twister have contracted some disease, or had someone terrified him? Puzzled, she climbed the steps to the back entrance. She decided she had to find Renegade in order to find the answer.

She pushed open the kitchen door and saw George, Bess, Peggy, and Tammy seated around the kitchen table. They all grinned when they saw Nancy. "About time you showed up," George said.

"Aren't you supposed to be in bed?" Nancy asked Tammy.

"That's right!" Peggy declared. "Dr. Hobart wouldn't like this."

Tammy sighed. "I know, but I couldn't sleep— not with Renegade out there!" Anxiously, she glanced through the window to the dark night beyond, and her hands shook a little as she cradled a cup of hot tea. "Hank was just here. He told us you followed Renegade to the ravine, and then he jumped and disappeared over the edge."

"That's the way it looked," Nancy admitted. She washed her hands, pulled up a chair, and joined her friends to tell them all about her adventure. Then Nancy persuaded Tammy to let her help her back to her room.

"I can't tell you how much I appreciate your help," Tammy said as she settled under the covers of her bed.

"I just wish I hadn't lost Renegade," Nancy said.

"We'll find him," Tammy whispered. Then she added, "We have to."

Nancy walked back to her room. After a long, hot shower, she knocked softly on the connecting door to the cousins' room.

"Come in," George called.

Nancy shoved the door open. George was flopped on her bed with a magazine, and Bess was busy painting her nails.

"Aren't you tired?" Nancy asked. Her muscles were beginning to ache from the long hours astride a horse.

"A little," George admitted, yawning. "Oh, with all the excitement about Renegade, I forgot to tell you the big news! While you were gone, Rob Majors phoned. I don't know what he said to Tammy, but she seemed pretty upset. When I asked her about it, she said it was nothing, just that he and that Landon guy are coming over here tomorrow."

"There's something else," Bess said, her blue eyes dancing.

"You two have been busy." Nancy smiled. "What's up?"

"Peggy told me that Mike Mathews is her nephew!" Bess said proudly.

"So what?" George asked.

Bess frowned. "Well, maybe nothing. But don't you think it's odd that Mike used to work for Nathaniel Baines, then ended up here? Why didn't he work here first, since his aunt has been with the Calloway Ranch for more than ten years?"

"Good question, Bess," Nancy said.

Bess blew on her nails. "And Peggy says the horses have been acting oddly for a week or so."

"So have some of the hands," Nancy said, then yawned. "They all act as if Twister's gone bad overnight." Her blue eyes glinted with determination. "But I'm going to prove them wrong."

"Uh-oh!" Bess glanced at George. "This time Nancy has really gone off her rocker. She's got a horse for a client!"

George groaned and tossed her magazine at Bess. "Good night, Nancy," she said with a wide grin.

"Good night," Nancy replied. She stretched one arm over her head and yawned, then walked back into her room and fell onto the bed. She was asleep the minute her head hit the pillow.

The next morning, after breakfast, Nancy, George, and Bess were leaning over a corral and watching Mike break one of the young trail horses. No matter how much the horse bucked or reared, he couldn't shake Mike.

"Mike was a bronco rider a few years ago,"

Bess explained. "Peggy said he won first prize in some of the local rodeos."

"Why did he quit?" Nancy asked.

Bess shrugged. "She didn't say. Maybe I should find out?"

"Good idea." Nancy eyed the stallion barn. She wanted to go back inside and investigate, but she knew she'd have to wait. Too many hands were in and out of the building, and she needed time to search Renegade's stall alone. "I wonder if Hank and Jimmy have found Renegade yet?" she asked, just as Stella Baines rode up on a long-legged bay mare.

Stella waved at Mike and tied her horse to the top rail of the fence. "Hi," she said brightly. "Is Tammy around?"

"In the house," Nancy said.

"I guess I'd better go in and tell her that Dad thinks he saw Renegade last night."

"Where?" Nancy, Bess, and George asked in unison.

"Over by the west end of our property early this morning. He was taking off for the hills," she said.

"How did you know he'd escaped?" Nancy asked.

Stella grinned at Mike as he rode up. "Hank West called." She glanced from Mike to the girls. "Of course, Dad wasn't sure it was Renegade, but it was a black stallion, big as life."

"Let's go!" Nancy said, turning toward the barns.

"Hey—wait!" Mike said. "Hank and one of the hands are already checking the hills."

"More eyes couldn't hurt," Nancy said.

Mike wiped the sweat from his forehead.

"Then I'm coming with you," he declared.

"Why don't you stay here with me?" Stella pouted.

Mike seemed torn. He looked at Stella fondly. "I've got a job to do," he reminded her. "Come on in while I tell Tammy."

Twenty minutes later, Nancy, George, and Mike rode to the west end of the Baines property. They searched together, but after several hours of scouring the hills at the west end of the Circle B, they finally gave up. "I just can't figure it," Mike said. "Where could he have gone?"

Nancy glanced at the endless hills. Trails wound through the thick woods in every direction. It would be easy for a horse to disappear. "I think we should talk to Mr. Baines himself," she suggested.

"You'd better let Tammy handle that," Mike said quickly.

"Why?"

He scowled. "Things have been strained between the two ranches for a few years. Competition has been tough. I don't think Nathaniel would appreciate one of the guests of the

Calloway Ranch poking around and asking questions. Let Tammy or Hank deal with him."

When they returned to the ranch, they discovered that Hank had returned, without Renegade. Hank had called Nathaniel Baines, who confirmed Stella's story.

"Nancy wants to talk with Baines," Mike told the ranch foreman.

Hank's lips thinned. "Look, Nancy, I know you're just trying to help, but I'd rather handle this on my own. Since Tammy's dad's death, I'm responsible. Besides, I don't want Nathaniel Baines to know there's any trouble over here."

"Why not?"

"Because he could make a big deal of it. If word gets around that we're losing horses or that some of our stock has gone bad, guests might prefer to stay at the Baines ranch. It's the last thing we need!" He turned and strode to the bunkhouse.

Later in the afternoon, against Dr. Hobart's orders, Tammy walked stiffly downstairs. Though pale and worried, she seemed much better than the night before.

"Let's have a glass of lemonade on the porch," she suggested to Nancy and her friends. "I can't stand lying in bed another minute!"

Soon they were all seated in chairs on the porch. Tammy took a sip from her glass and sighed. "I told Hank to call the sheriff's office," she said to Nancy. "That way, if anyone sees Renegade, we'll be notified."

Nancy was relieved. "Good. Have you talked with Nathaniel Baines?"

"Yes, but I don't think he saw Renegade." As if reading the questions in Nancy's eyes, Tammy said, "Oh, he wasn't lying. But the horse he saw sounded too much like a range horse—a wild mustang. It was too short and unkempt to be Renegade."

"One more dead end," George murmured, glancing toward the long drive at the sound of a car's engine. "Uh-oh. Just what we need. More trouble."

A long white car raced down the lane and slammed to a stop only a few feet from the porch.

At the sight of the car, Tammy turned even paler.

Rob Majors parked, then swaggered up the steps to the porch. He glanced at Nancy and her friends before saying to Tammy, "I see you're on your feet again."

"Almost," Tammy replied stiffly.

Vern Landon sauntered onto the porch behind Rob Majors. He tipped his wide Stetson toward Nancy and her friends, but his eyes remained cold and distant. "I'd like to make an offer on this place," he said, reaching into his inner jacket pocket and withdrawing a checkbook. "Is there somewhere we can talk privately?"

"We don't need to," Tammy said coldly. "I'm not interested."

"But you haven't heard the price." Vern Landon's face hardened.

"It doesn't matter," Tammy retorted. "This place was my grandfather's, my father's, and now it's mine. I won't sell this place just so that it can be turned into some resort filled with condominiums. Not for any price."

"That's not very smart," Rob Majors warned.

Tammy struggled to her feet. "I told you I'd make the back payments—on the fifth of July."

"You're in no condition to ride in a rodeo," Rob Majors pointed out.

"I will be," Tammy said, suddenly angry. "Just watch. Meanwhile, thank you, gentlemen, but get off my ranch. Now!"

6

A Silver Buckle

Tammy turned and marched into the house, banging the screen door behind her.

"That was your last chance!" Vern Landon yelled after her.

"Stupid woman!" Rob Majors said gruffly. He looked at the three friends. "If you have any influence with Tammy," he said, "you'd better tell her to listen to Landon's offer. As far as I'm concerned, it's her only hope of getting anything out of this place! I heard she lost her prize stallion."

"Bad news travels fast," George observed.

Majors pressed his lips together angrily. "Without that stallion, she has nothing but a dried-up dust bowl and a few sagging buildings. The bank is ready to close this place. Time is running out."

Nancy remembered Renegade's value as a stallion. Tammy was counting on Renegade's foals in the future.

Rob started down the steps, then stopped, turning to look at Nancy. A cold smile slid over his lips. "And by the way, I don't believe that horse escaped. I just bet Tammy engineered the entire fiasco."

"Why would she do that?" Bess asked indignantly.

Rob Majors glanced at Landon. "For the insurance money," he said. "That horse was worth a bundle. But she won't get away with it! I personally guarantee that the insurance company will find out about her scam. And when they find that she set the whole thing up, they'll close this place down and lock her up!"

Nancy watched as the two men climbed back into the car.

"Nice guys," George observed.

"Why does he want this place so badly? There must be other ranches for sale," Nancy mused.

"Maybe not in Misty Canyon."

"I wonder." Deciding she couldn't stand waiting around any longer, Nancy said, "I'm going to check on the ridge where Renegade jumped last night. Anyone want to join me?"

"Sure," George agreed.

Bess shook her head. "I promised Peggy I'd help in the kitchen this afternoon."

"Good. You can cover for us," Nancy said.

"What will we do if we run into Hank?" George asked as they headed for the barns.

"I don't know. I guess we'll have to cross that *ridge* when we come to it."

Chuckling, George grabbed two bridles from the tack room.

On the ridge, nothing had changed. Nancy studied the dust prints and found her own boot-heel marks and Renegade's hoofprints. She could see where he'd jumped over the edge of the creek and where he'd landed on the bank, but his prints didn't show up on the far side of the stream.

"He must have disappeared," George said, wiping beads of sweat from her forehead.

"Or galloped up or down the creek." Nancy walked each way but couldn't find any trace of the horse.

"Only fish follow streams," George said, her eyes sweeping the landscape of brush and pine trees. "Or convicts who want to destroy their scent so dogs can't follow them."

"What about horses that are ridden to cover their tracks?"

"Oh, yeah, right. The horse no man can ride

70

was ridden through a dark forest, over a cliff, and up a creek."

Even Nancy had to admit her theory was farfetched. But something she couldn't put her finger on bothered her. She checked the surrounding brush but couldn't find another clue —not one scrap of cloth caught on a branch, no strand of horse hair wound around a twig, no evidence along the muddy shores.

"Maybe Hank has found Renegade by now," George said, but she didn't sound convinced.

They rode back to the ranch and found Bess in the kitchen with Tammy. As they shared a soda, the friends listened to Tammy's fascinating stories about rodeo riding. Tammy had won bareback races as well as performing as a trick rider.

"It sounds glamorous!" Bess exclaimed.

"More like hard work, if you ask me," George said.

Nancy glanced out the window and spied Hank West and Jimmy Robbins near the stallion barns. But Renegade wasn't with them. Tammy followed Nancy's gaze as Hank handed the reins of his horse to Jimmy and walked up the back steps.

"So you didn't find him," Tammy said anxiously as he entered the kitchen.

"No. It beats me where that devil horse could have gone." Hank mopped his dusty brow with a red handkerchief. His face was grimy and weathered from the sun as he glanced at Nancy. "Don't suppose you went looking for him, now, did you, Nancy? Those weren't *your* tracks by the stream, were they?"

"Nancy was only trying to help," Tammy said quickly. "I asked her to. Did you reach the sheriff's office?"

Hank sighed. "I haven't called them yet."

Tammy was flabbergasted. "Why not?"

"Because it wouldn't do any good, that's why," he blurted out. "Calling the sheriff would just give us more bad publicity around here."

"But if someone sees him—"

"I've called the neighboring ranches," Hank said, his face softening as he spoke to Tammy. "Don't worry. We'll find him."

"I hope so," Tammy said, twisting her hands in her lap.

After dinner, as the guests were getting ready for canoe races that evening, Nancy sensed an opportunity to check for clues in the stallion barn. Though the sun hadn't set yet, activity had slowed at the ranch. Some of the hands had the evening off and were in town. Calloway Ranch was quiet. "Cover for me," Nancy whispered to George.

"What're you doing?"

"I'll join you in a few minutes. I just want to

check out Renegade's stall when no one else is around."

Moving like a shadow, Nancy ducked into the stallion barn. Several horses nickered. The barn was dim, but she didn't want to turn on the lights. Reaching into her jacket pocket, she pulled out her flashlight and switched it on.

Renegade's stall looked just the same as it had earlier. No clue there. Cautiously, she swept the beam of her flashlight along the cement floor, the dusty rafters, and the walls. There was nothing out of the ordinary. Then she quickly searched the stalls next to Renegade's. Horses whinnied and scraped metal-shod hooves against the cement.

Nancy checked her watch and realized she'd already been away from the group for fifteen minutes. She had to join the others before she was missed.

Sighing, Nancy turned to leave but stopped short at Twister's stall. The stallion was restless and pawing angrily.

The hairs on the back of Nancy's neck stood on end. Was he anxious because of her—or was someone else in the building? She clicked off her flashlight and held her breath to listen.

She heard the sounds of laughter from the bunkhouse, the rustle of hooves against straw, and the agitated noises coming from Twister. But nothing in the stallion barn.

After a few seconds, she breathed again and clicked on her flashlight. She peered into Twister's stall. The horse's ears were flattened, his nostrils flared, and he stepped back. Nancy trained her light away from his face and onto his legs, but he started to rear.

She heard a noise behind her. Her pulse jumped. Startled, she turned just as she felt a jarring blow to the back of her head. At the same instant, she felt the stall door give way. Lights flashed behind her eyes as she stumbled into Twister's stall.

She turned to face her attacker in horror. A silver belt buckle was slamming at her face! She tried to jump aside, but the blow landed with a sickening thud.

Nancy crumpled to the ground, unconscious, as the stallion reared above her.

7

Accused!

"Nancy! Nancy!"

George's voice sounded distant. Nancy tried to open her eyes but felt a jab of pain sear through her brain. "George?" she whispered, forcing her eyes open. Under the bright lights in the aisle of the stallion barn, Bess and George knelt beside Nancy.

"Thank goodness you're awake! What happened?" Bess asked.

Nancy rubbed the back of her head. "Someone hit me."

"Who?" George demanded.

Wincing, Nancy shook her head. "I don't

know. All I saw was a silver belt buckle. But I was *in* Twister's stall. The stall door gave way, and I fell inside when I was hit."

Bess said, "The stall door is closed now. And that horse is inside."

"Whoever hit me must have pulled me to safety," said Nancy.

"Well, that's something," George murmured. "Stay here, and I'll go get Dr. Hobart."

"No! Really—I feel better already." It was the truth. As Nancy's eyes adjusted to the light, the pounding in her head subsided. She pushed herself upright, and her head cleared.

"You're sure?" George asked skeptically.

"Positive. I'll just have a headache for a while."

"It wouldn't hurt to have the doctor look at it," George insisted. She snapped out the lights, and the three friends walked out of the stallion barn. An evening breeze lifted Nancy's hair off her face.

"You know what this means, don't you? Someone doesn't like my investigating," Nancy said.

"But who?" George asked.

"That's the big question," Nancy said. "It couldn't have been Mike Mathews. He was at the lake for the canoe races."

"But he was gone for more than ten minutes," George said. "We had to wait for him."

"Why?"

"Oh, he went to the bunkhouse and came back

with some safety equipment—extra life preservers and some flares. His girlfriend, Stella, was with him. And her father. They came to ask about Renegade, but they've already left."

"Wonderful," Nancy said, frowning. "What about Hank West?"

Bess shook her head. "He had a quick cup of coffee with Peggy, then left because he had work to do. I tried to stop him by offering him another piece of pie, but he wasn't interested."

"Great. Just when I start investigating, practically every suspect I have shows up," Nancy said, discouraged.

"Oh, Nancy," George said with a grin. "Whoever said detective work was easy?"

The next morning, Nancy showered early and threw on blue jeans, a T-shirt, and running shoes. She was on her way to breakfast when Tammy caught up with her.

"Dr. Hobart says I'm okay," Tammy announced.

"That's good news!"

"The best. Now I can start training again." She flashed a bright smile.

They walked downstairs together, and Tammy paused at the front door. "How would you like to help me with chores this morning?" she asked. "You can see how the hands care for the stock."

"I'd love it," Nancy said.

They toured the barns, making sure that all the cattle and horses were fed and had plenty of water. As they walked outside, Nancy had to squint against the bright sunshine. Already the day was warm. On a hunch, Nancy asked, "Where do you keep the medication for the horses?"

"Mostly in the tack room. There's a cabinet in a corner."

"What do you keep in there?"

"All the veterinary supplies—vitamins, ointment, liniment, anything we might need in case of an injury." She glanced at Nancy with quizzical green eyes. "Why do you ask?"

"I just wondered if Twister's change in temperament might be because he's been drugged."

Tammy laughed. "I don't think so. Who would do that?"

"Anyone who wants you out of the rodeo," Nancy said.

Sobering, Tammy said, "That's an awful thought. No one would hurt one of the horses just to keep me from riding!"

"It's possible, Tammy," Nancy said. "And maybe that same person stole Renegade."

"Stole him? But he escaped—Mike saw him take off."

"Mike only saw him before he galloped out of the barn. When I was chasing Renegade, I thought I saw someone on his back."

"But it was dark."

"That's why I wasn't sure," Nancy said.

Tammy shook her head, and her red hair glinted in the morning sun. "I can't believe that one, Nancy. No one can ride Renegade. Come on, let's have breakfast. Then we can ride out to the ridge. I want to see where Renegade disappeared."

The creek cut a silvery swath beneath the ridge. Nancy, Tammy, George, and Bess stared down at the rushing water from the edge of the cliff.

"You mean he actually leapt over this and into the water?" Bess asked, her eyes rounding. "Wouldn't he have been hurt?"

"He could have been," Tammy said, her brows drawing together under the brim of her Stetson. "But Renegade's pretty surefooted." She slid from the saddle of her roan gelding and studied the land. "But where is he? He's a smart horse. Even if he were spooked or wanted to run away, he'd come back."

"Unless he was stolen," Nancy ventured.

"Why would anyone steal him?"

"Didn't you say he was the most valuable asset of the ranch?" Nancy asked, thinking back to Rob Majors's remarks about Renegade's worth.

Tammy's eyes narrowed. "That's impossible," she decided. "If anyone wanted to steal him, he'd have to be able to handle him, and only a few hands at our ranch can even get near him." She swung back onto her horse, and the girls returned to the ranch just in time to clean up for lunch.

After the meal, Nancy decided it was time to visit Nathaniel Baines, in spite of Hank's objections, and question him about the horse he'd seen on his property. "Anyone want to join me?" she asked, poking her head into Bess and George's room.

"Can't we do it later?" Bess asked as she brushed her hair into a ponytail. "George and I were thinking about walking over to the lake and taking a swim."

Nancy had to admit that a cool swim at the lake on the edge of Tammy's property, near the Circle B, sounded refreshing. But she had work to do. She went downstairs.

As she headed across the yard, Nancy saw two of the guests marching to the paddock, where Tammy was riding the roan gelding. They were red-faced and waving angrily.

"I wonder what's going on?" Nancy murmured to herself. She ran toward the corral to see what was happening.

Tammy was on one side of the fence, the two furious guests on the other. The man shouted, "I don't care what you have to do, Miss Calloway, but we're reporting the theft to the police!"

"Theft?" Nancy repeated.

"That's right!" the woman declared. "Someone stole my purse and my husband's wallet!"

"You're sure?" Tammy asked nervously.

The woman's eyes glittered dangerously. "Of course I'm sure! They were both in the bureau drawer until this morning! One of those cowboys must have come in and stolen them!"

Tammy's face was ashen. "I can assure you, Mrs. Mason, all of our hands are above suspicion."

"Then who took them?" the woman screamed.

Nancy heard the screen door slam and looked up to find Peggy Holgate running from the kitchen. Her face was drawn into lines of worry. "Are these what you're looking for?" she asked, holding up a leather wallet and a small clutch purse.

"Yes!" Mrs. Mason snatched the purse and wallet from Peggy's outstretched fingers. "Where did you find them?"

Peggy hesitated. She glanced nervously at Nancy, then to Tammy. "I was just cleaning Nancy's room," she said slowly. "Her duffel bag was on the bed, so I moved it, and the wallet and purse fell out."

"What?" Nancy gasped.

"So you're the culprit!" Mrs. Mason accused, her face flushed in anger as she glared at Nancy. "Well, don't think you're getting away with it! I intend to call the police and have you arrested, Nancy Drew!"

8

Clue in the Chronicle

Shocked, Nancy said, "I don't know how your things got into my room!"

Bess and George ran up and heard the end of the conversation.

"Nancy wouldn't steal anything!" George said indignantly. "It's obvious she's been framed! Nancy's bag has her name on it!"

Mrs. Mason rummaged in her purse, checking the contents, then relaxed a little. "Everything's still here, but I won't forget this," she said as her husband counted the bills in his wallet.

"We'll get to the bottom of it," Tammy promised, but her voice shook a little.

As the husband and wife walked stiff-backed toward the house, Tammy confided, "Nothing like this has ever happened at the ranch before. I don't understand it."

"I do," Bess said. "Nancy must be getting too close to the truth about what happened to Renegade!"

Peggy touched Nancy's arm. "I didn't want to point a finger at you," she said anxiously. "I know you didn't take anything."

Nancy gave the housekeeper a kind smile. "It's okay. We'll figure this out."

"I hope so," Tammy whispered.

Peggy glanced at her watch and gasped, "Look at the time! I've got to start getting things ready for the barbecue tonight!"

"Do you need some help?" Bess offered, glancing at George. "My cousin and I are a fabulous team in the kitchen."

George started to protest. "Well, I'm not the greatest—"

"I could use all the help I can get. And I know all about your skills in the kitchen from your mother," Peggy said to George.

"I'll be right with you," Nancy promised as George and Bess followed Peggy to the house.

Tammy said, "I'm sorry about Mrs. Mason."

Nancy sighed. "Don't worry—I've been accused of worse. Besides, this just helps to prove my theory. Someone's trying to stop my investigation—whoever it is must be getting nervous. Do you have any idea who might have helped Renegade escape?"

"You really don't think he just took off?"

"Do you?"

Tammy shrugged. "I did. But he's been gone so long without a trace."

Nancy's mind was working quickly. "It seems to me that either Renegade escaped on his own and someone found him and took advantage of the fact that he was missing. Or someone actually let him out."

"Someone, meaning Mike Mathews?" Tammy asked, chewing on her lower lip.

"Maybe. Or someone who doesn't want you to ride in the Independence Day Rodeo," Nancy said. "I think that Renegade's disappearance and Twister's change in temperament are related."

"But how?"

"I don't know yet. But without Renegade as a breeding stallion and without Twister to ride in the rodeo, you won't be able to pay back that loan."

"I know." Tammy sighed.

Nancy leaned her back against the top rail of the fence. "I heard Vern Landon tell Rob Majors that he'd get this ranch from you one way or another."

"You think he's behind it?"

Nancy shrugged. "I'd like to find out more about him."

Tammy made a face. "The less I know of him, the better. He gives me the creeps." She shivered. "I would never sell this ranch to him." She stared at the cloudless sky. "Tonight, at the barbecue, I'm going to make an official announcement that my retirement is over," she said, her chin thrust forward. "I just wish we could find Renegade."

"We will," Nancy promised. "I plan on riding over to the Circle B and asking Nathaniel Baines about the horse he spotted."

"Don't bother," Tammy said. "That stallion was just a range horse, not Renegade."

"I'd still like to talk to Baines."

"You'll get your chance tonight. I invited him, Stella, and a few other neighbors to the barbecue." She slapped the top rail of the fence and added, "I've got to check on some of the calves. I'll see you later."

Nancy started for the house. Once she was in the main yard, she changed directions when she saw Mike Mathews walk from the stallion barn. He took a quick look over his shoulder, then climbed into the Calloway Ranch station wagon and drove off. Nancy decided to look around in the stallion barn one more time.

Inside, the barn was dark, quiet, and musty-smelling. All of the horses were outside.

Nancy walked straight to Renegade's stall. Nothing had changed—the white-gold straw was still messed, the manger half full, the water bucket hung on its hook, and the rails of the gate hadn't been repaired. She started to turn away but felt as if she were missing something. Her gaze swept the stall. Everything was just where it was before—or was it?

Frowning, she stared at Twister's stall. It, too, seemed the same, except that the straw had been changed and seemed a darker shade of gold.

Nancy had a feeling there was a valuable clue in the stallion barn, one she was overlooking. Still lost in thought, Nancy walked back to the main house, where she found Bess and George in the kitchen.

"Did you bring your camera?" Bess asked, cocking her head in George's direction.

George, covered in a long white apron, was attacking onions with a vengeance. "Take that— and that," she joked as she diced the vegetables with quick strokes.

Chopped meat was sizzling in a large saucepan. Peggy was busy creating her special homemade chili, while Bess was pouring thick cornbread batter into cake pans.

"Anything I can do?" Nancy offered.

"Take over for me," George grumbled.

"You can get the corn in the pantry and husk it

for me," Peggy suggested, looking over her shoulder as she stirred tomato sauce and beans into the meat.

"Okay!" Nancy walked through the kitchen to the pantry just off the back porch. The corn was in one bin, and as Nancy reached for several of the silk-tasseled ears, she knocked over a stack of yellowed newspapers piled high in a corner.

"Clumsy Nancy," she murmured to herself. She straightened the scattered papers before gathering the corn.

Half an hour later, dinner was well under way. Hank West strode into the kitchen. "Tammy around?" he asked, lines of worry grooving his face.

"I think she's upstairs," Peggy replied.

"Not anymore." Tammy walked into the kitchen wearing black jeans, a red-and-white-checked shirt, and a scarlet hat.

"I thought you'd want to know," Hank said. "We couldn't find a trace of Renegade. I'm afraid he's gone for good."

Tammy slumped into one of the kitchen chairs. "I can't believe it," she murmured.

"Neither can I," Hank admitted. "I finally did call the sheriff's office and every neighbor again, within ten miles. No one's seen him."

"He's got to be hidden somewhere," Nancy said.

"Oh, does he now?" Hank asked, one silvery brow arching suspiciously as he faced Nancy. "Where?"

"I don't know," Nancy answered, "but I think someone's deliberately hiding him."

"That's the craziest notion you've come up with yet," Hank said, his temper exploding. "I don't know how you solve crimes in the city, Nancy Drew, but out here we wait until something is stolen before we try to prove who did it!"

"That's just it! Nancy thinks Renegade *was* stolen," Tammy explained.

"Merciful heavens!" Peggy declared.

Hank's eyes registered disbelief. "He took off. That's all."

"Then why haven't we found him?" Nancy challenged. "Unless he's been hidden, he would've turned up by now."

"Bah!" Shaking his head, Hank turned and left the room.

Peggy glanced from one girl to the other. "I, uh, think I can handle this myself," she said, gesturing to the food. "You girls run along and get cleaned up for the barbecue."

George removed her apron gratefully, but Bess lingered in the kitchen. "I'll be up soon," she told Nancy.

A few minutes later, Nancy opened the connecting door to the cousins' room. She'd already changed into fresh jeans and a western shirt with pearl buttons. Flopping onto Bess's bed, she said, "I have this feeling that I'm missing something— something important."

"You?" George grinned. "I doubt it."

Nancy rested her chin in her hand. "If only I could figure out who stole Renegade and planted the Masons' things in my bag."

"And how Twister's been drugged?" George asked.

"*If* he's been drugged," Nancy said in vexation. "So far, we can't prove that, either."

"So where are we?" George asked. She was brushing her short dark hair and watching Nancy in the reflection of the bureau mirror.

"Back to square one."

The door suddenly burst open, and Bess, her blue eyes shining, flew into the room. "I know who the culprit is!" she whispered loudly as she closed the door. "I know who's behind everything—and I can prove it!"

9

This Party's a Blast

"Who?" Nancy and George asked together.

"Mike Mathews!" Bess said. She dug into the pocket of her apron and pulled out a yellowed page from the local newspaper, the *Chronicle*. Triumphantly, she held it toward Nancy.

George read over Nancy's shoulder: "Local Bronc Buster Busted Himself."

The story was six months old and reported that Mike Mathews had been convicted of stealing from guests at the ranch where he worked—the Circle B! He had been fired by Nathaniel Baines, who owned the popular ranch and was father to Stella Baines, a famous bareback rider. The Circle B was known for its prize rodeo stock and small zoo of exotic reptiles.

"How'd you find out about this?" George asked.

Bess sat on the edge of her bed and smiled in satisfaction. "In those old newspapers in the pantry. The headline caught my eye."

George looked thoughtful. "Why would Mike Mathews let Renegade escape? What would he get out of it?"

"Isn't Stella Baines his girlfriend?" Bess asked.

Nancy brightened. "That's right. And if Tammy enters the Independence Day Rodeo, Stella might lose the bareback riding contest! It's worth a lot of money. The winner will be awarded a big commercial contract."

"Peggy told me that the rodeo was going to be on national television," George added. "And some of the winning contestants might be offered a part in a movie."

"So it's worth a lot of money," Nancy thought aloud, "as well as fame."

"Maybe Mike is sabotaging Tammy's chances because he's in love with Stella," Bess murmured.

"*If* he's sabotaging anything at all," Nancy remarked. "Remember—we still don't have any proof."

George grinned crookedly and squared a

turquoise-colored Stetson on her head. "Then let's go find some."

"Where?" Bess asked. "At the barbecue?"

"For starters," Nancy said, thinking ahead. "I can't wait to talk to Mike Mathews *and* Nathaniel Baines!"

An hour later, the smells of tangy barbecue sauce, fresh-baked cornbread, and strawberry pie filled the air. Guests gathered around the open pit where the char-blackened beef was sizzling. Lanterns flickered in the spreading branches of the trees overhead, and conversation buzzed through the throng.

Nancy, Bess, and George joined the guests and neighbors of Calloway Ranch. As she filled her plate, Nancy searched the crowd, her gaze moving over the faces of the people she knew until she found Stella Baines.

Stella's platinum hair shone beneath the lanterns. She was standing next to a tall, heavyset man with big jowls, a deep laugh, and silver white hair.

"Here I go," Nancy whispered to Bess as she wended her way through the guests toward Stella. "Hi," she said, waving at the pretty rodeo queen.

"Hi—Nancy, isn't it?" Stella asked. She stared at Nancy as if she barely recognized her.

"Right." Nancy glanced up at the big man.

"I'm Nathaniel Baines, Stella's father," he said, his voice booming as he extended his hand and clasped Nancy's palm in a firm grip. "Welcome to Montana!"

"Thank you."

"I hear you're a detective of some sort."

Stella shot him an anxious look.

"Of some sort," Nancy replied with a bright smile. "I've been trying to find Renegade. He escaped the other night."

"So I heard," Nathaniel remarked. "Stella said something about it, and I thought I saw him on the west end of my property. But I guess I was wrong. That horse was just a range stallion. Don't know how I could've made such a mistake. Renegade's pretty distinctive—except when he's near Twister. I can't tell those two apart."

"Nobody can," Mike Mathews said as he joined the group. Nancy turned toward him, and she nearly gasped. He was wearing jeans, a plaid shirt, and a belt with a silver buckle—a buckle just like the one she had seen before she was knocked out in the barn! She wondered now if Mike had been her attacker. She couldn't be sure. Lots of ranch hands wore silver buckles, and she still didn't have any proof that he was involved in Renegade's disappearance.

Nathaniel Baines's face grew hard as he stared at the young ranch hand, but Mike met the older man's gaze steadily.

"Your friend George is looking for you," Mike said to Nancy. He sent Stella an affectionate glance before walking quickly away.

Nancy excused herself from Nathaniel and Stella but didn't go to look for George. Instead, she followed Mike as he strode toward the stables. "Wait a minute," Nancy called.

Mike stopped short and turned on the heel of his boot. "Your friend is back at the party," he said curtly.

"I know," Nancy said. "But I wanted to talk to you."

He faced her but didn't seem interested. "What about?"

"The other night, when I was in the stallion barn—"

"I remember," he cut in. "You were asking all sorts of questions while I was trying to calm Twister down."

"No—later. I was in the stallion barn alone."

"That's dangerous," he said, exploding. "Especially in the state Twister's in!"

Nancy didn't give up. "That's the night you were supposed to be at the canoe races."

His jaw tightened, and his eyes narrowed a fraction. "That's right. What were you doing in the barn?"

"Looking for clues," she explained.

"Oh, right. I've heard you think Renegade was

94

stolen." He laughed and shook his head. "There's no mystery here, Nancy, so quit trying to create one."

"I was knocked out that night," she said boldly. "Someone came up behind me and hit me on the back of the head."

Mike's laughter died. "This is crazy. I never heard about any attack!"

"I decided it would be best to keep it quiet."

He seemed about to argue but finally asked, "What happened?"

"My friends found me."

"Did you see your attacker?"

"No. But as I was falling to the floor, I did catch a glimpse of a silver buckle—a buckle just like yours."

Mike's jaw worked angrily. "So you think maybe I knocked you out?" He pointed to his belt. "This buckle was a prize I won at a local rodeo a few years back. Everyone who wins at the county fair gets one. A dozen people here tonight have one."

"Who?" Nancy prodded.

"Tammy, Jimmy, and Hank, for starters," he said, thinking. "A couple of the stable hands, too. And that doesn't count the hands from other ranches in the area."

"Like the Circle B?" Nancy asked, her mind leaping ahead.

His brows drew together over his eyes. "I suppose a few of the guys who work for Nathaniel Baines have won."

"How about Stella?" Nancy asked, remembering the first time she'd met Stella. She had been wearing a silver buckle then.

Mike's eyes softened a little. "She's got several," he allowed. Then his voice grew bitter. "So does her old man."

Great, Nancy thought. If what Mike is saying is true, half the people in the county have buckles like the one I saw!

Mike started toward the barns. "Look, I've really got to feed the stock—"

"Just one more thing," Nancy said quickly. "You used to work for Nathaniel Baines, didn't you?"

Mike stopped dead in his tracks. Every muscle in his body tensed as he turned. "How'd you know about that?" he demanded.

"I read about it in the papers."

"Ancient history," Mike muttered. Then he scowled angrily. "Big deal! You probably know I did a little time for theft."

"Mr. Baines is probably disappointed it wasn't more."

Mike clenched his fists. "There's no love lost between me and Baines. He never liked me. He didn't think I was good enough for Stella. He still doesn't. When he found out about the things I'd lifted off the guests, he fired me on the spot, pressed charges, and told me never to see Stella again."

Nancy saw his anger become hatred. "So you got a job here?"

"Hey, look, it's not like Tammy was thrilled with me. She just took me on as a hard-luck case. My aunt talked her into it." His eyes glittered. "I've been straight, trying to prove to Aunt Peggy, Tammy, and the whole state that I've turned over a new leaf."

Nancy wasn't quite ready to trust him. "So you don't know why the Masons' things were stolen and left in my room?"

"You think *I* was involved in that?" he asked incredulously. "Are you out of your mind? This might not be the best job around, but I'm not about to blow it now. Besides, nothing was really stolen, right? The Masons' money wasn't touched."

"Someone tried to frame me," Nancy pointed out.

"Well, it wasn't me! Now, if that's all—" He stomped furiously away toward the stables.

Nancy watched him disappear through the door. Was he telling the truth? He'd been convicted of theft before. Would he steal Renegade? But what about Twister? Mike seemed to genuinely like horses. Would he drug the stallion or terrify Twister in some manner? Or was Hank West right—had Twister gone bad? Where was Renegade? Somewhere up in the hills—or hidden in a private barn?

"You look like you're a million miles away," Bess observed as Nancy rejoined the party.

"Not that far," Nancy replied. "I was just thinking that maybe it was time to visit some of the neighboring ranches and speak with the owners."

Tammy caught the end of Nancy's conversation. "Most of them are here," she said, pointing out Mr. and Mrs. Franklin, who owned the ranch south of Calloway's, and Edna Peterkin, a widow who owned the spread to the west of the Circle B.

Nancy mingled with the guests, speaking with each person. She learned nothing—only that none of the neighboring ranchers had seen Renegade.

But Edna Peterkin said, "You mark my words— even though Renegade is a devil, I'll bet he liked being fed twice a day. Out there"—she crooked her thumb toward the hills—"the pickings are slim. Horses are smart, mostly too smart to just disappear. Oh, listen, the band's tuning up."

On a platform near the back porch of the main house, three country musicians had begun warming up. Nancy moved closer to the stage, where Tammy was talking with Stella Baines. "You're really going to go back to riding?" Stella asked just as Nancy joined them.

"It looks that way. I plan to start on Independence Day."

"Isn't that a little soon?" Stella asked. "You haven't been in a rodeo for more than a year."

"The prize money and commercial endorsements are worth it."

"Worth risking your life on that crazy horse?" Stella asked.

"Twister's not crazy—"

"Hank's been talking with my father, and Mike even said that Twister has turned bad," Stella insisted. "I wouldn't trust a horse that's unpredictable." Without a backward glance, she walked haughtily away.

"What was that all about?" Tammy asked.

"I'd like to know, too," Nancy murmured, watching as Stella linked her arm through Mike's. Nathaniel Baines was close by, and he scowled when he saw his daughter with his ex-employee. "I heard that Mike used to work for the Circle B."

Tammy nodded. "Do you know why he was fired?"

"Yes."

"I see," Tammy said, grimacing. "I guess I should have told you that he had stolen from guests at the Circle B, but I really don't think Mike had anything to do with Renegade's disappearance or the Masons' stolen purse and wallet. Since nothing was taken, I didn't see any reason to dredge up Mike's past."

The band started playing a favorite country ballad, and Tammy said, "That's my cue. After this song, I'm going to announce the end of my retirement."

"Good luck," Nancy said encouragingly. Then she saw something from the corner of her eye. "Uh-oh."

"What?" Tammy followed Nancy's gaze to the lane, where a long white sedan rolled toward the ranch house. It was Rob Majors's car. "Not again," Tammy muttered.

The car slowed to a stop, and Rob Majors left the engine idling as he climbed from behind the steering wheel. Vern Landon peered through the passenger-side window but didn't open his door. Majors walked briskly past the barbecue pits, beneath the swinging lanterns, and straight to Tammy.

"I told you this would happen," he said, slapping a thick envelope into her palm.

"What's this?" Tammy asked.

"I'm calling the loan. You have one month to pay everything back or clear out."

"You can't do this!" Tammy exclaimed as the music died and all the eyes of the guests turned toward Tammy and the banker.

"Sure I can," Rob taunted. "Read it, and don't

forget the fine print. By the way, I called the insurance company. They told me they weren't about to pay you for Renegade. They don't believe he's dead, injured, or stolen. They think you've got him hidden somewhere!"

Tammy's shoulders stiffened. "I haven't talked to anyone at the insurance company!"

"Well, I wouldn't even try, because they're on to you." He turned on his heel and strode back to his car.

"What was that all about?" George asked, coming up to Nancy.

"I don't know," she said, "but I'm going to find out."

Peggy hurried up to Tammy. "There's been a mix-up! Mike forgot to pick up the soda at the store this afternoon. Just drove off and left it! And I'm all out of iced tea. Thank goodness I was able to reach the grocer. Carl Williams said he'd keep the store open until we pick up the pop."

Tammy surveyed the hot crowd. "It'll only take twenty minutes or so. I'll go."

"No, you stay here," Nancy insisted. "I'll drive."

"Would you?" Tammy seemed relieved.

"It's Williams Market, just this side of town," Peggy explained. "He'll be waiting for you."

Tammy fished into the pockets of her jeans. "Take my station wagon," she offered, then motioned to the band. The lead singer nodded, and a few seconds later the strains of another country ballad filled the night.

"I'll be right back," Nancy said, pocketing Tammy's keys.

"What're you planning?" George asked Nancy.

"I'm just running an errand for Tammy. There's been a mix-up with the drinks. Want to come along?"

"Sure."

They told Bess what they were going to do, then dashed across the yard to the battered old station wagon parked far from the festivities. The car was painted with Calloway Ranch's logo—a big green *C* and a black stallion.

"I wonder if Mike just made a mistake with the soda—or if it was intentional."

"Why would he?" George asked.

"Beats me," Nancy said, climbing into the car. "Maybe just to cause more trouble." She flicked on the ignition.

The engine coughed, then caught. Nancy put the car into reverse. The car shimmied strangely. Warning bells went off in Nancy's head. She grabbed George with one hand and tried to open the door with the other. "Let's get out of—"

Before she could finish, an ear-splitting blast ripped through the metal frame.

10

Hiss!

Nancy and George shoved open the car doors and leapt to the ground. "Run!" Nancy yelled.

They scrambled to their feet, raced across the yard, and climbed up a grassy embankment away from the car. Gasping for breath, Nancy turned and saw orange and red sparks shoot high into the sky. Black smoke billowed from the hood. Horrified guests ran in all directions.

"That was too close for comfort," George murmured shakily.

Hank West ran from the tack room, carrying a fire extinguisher. "Out of the way!" he yelled at people blocking his path as he sprayed the car. He shouted more commands to some of the hands who had gathered near the blazing station wagon.

"Nancy! George!" Bess ran up to them. "Are you okay?"

"We'll survive," George replied.

"What happened?" Bess was pale, her eyes round.

"I don't know." Nancy shook her head and watched as Mike Mathews ran from the stables with another fire extinguisher. Jimmy Robbins turned a large gardening hose onto the burning car. A few minutes later, the flames were reduced to smoldering, charred metal. "I stepped on the gas pedal, and something went wrong." She frowned. "It was just like a bomb."

"No!" Bess cried, clamping a hand over her mouth.

Tammy sprinted across the gravel-strewn yard to the hill where Nancy, George, and Bess were huddled together. Peggy Holgate was right on Tammy's heels.

"Are you all right?" Tammy asked anxiously, eyeing George and Nancy.

"I think so," Nancy replied.

"You were lucky. I can't imagine what went wrong," Tammy said. "The car was fine when Mike went into town for groceries."

"Has anyone used it since?" Nancy asked.

Tammy shook her head. "No. He gave the keys back to me."

Nancy frowned thoughtfully at the car. "I think someone put some sort of bomb under the station wagon."

"No!" Tammy cried. "Why would someone want to hurt you?"

"Not me," Nancy said slowly. "Who usually drives the car?"

"I do," Tammy started, "but—"

"Then it looks like you were the target."

Tammy closed her eyes, and Nancy placed a steadying arm around her shoulders. "I can't believe it," Tammy said.

"Seems like there's more than enough proof," George pointed out, gesturing toward the charred body of the car.

Bess shuddered. "This is getting serious!"

"Someone has to call the police," Nancy said.

"I called the police and fire departments when the car exploded," Peggy explained. "They should be here soon."

A few minutes later, Nancy heard the wail of distant sirens. A fire truck and a car from the sheriff's department raced into the yard. Firefighters jumped to the ground and ran to the car.

Detectives started asking everyone questions.

"Didn't you see anyone hanging around the car earlier?" a red-faced deputy named Dennis McMillan asked Nancy and Tammy.

"No—" Tammy began.

Mike Mathews sauntered up. "I drove that car

into town this afternoon. I parked it right there, near the stables."

"And you didn't have any trouble with it?" Deputy McMillan asked.

"None at all." Mike's face was drawn, and beneath his tan, his skin seemed to have whitened.

"It was fireworks," one firefighter cut in as he approached the deputy. He was holding a blackened casing. "This was lit on a long fuse and rolled under the front of the car. I think it caught fire on oil dripping from the engine."

"Then it could have been an accident?" Tammy asked.

The fireman shook his head. "A prank that went bad, maybe. But I doubt it." His eyes were serious.

"That does it," Tammy decided solemnly. She turned to Nancy. "You're off the case. I can't have you taking any more risks!"

"Case?" Deputy McMillan asked. "What case?"

Nancy explained about the missing horse.

The officer snorted. "Well, a stallion's disappearance isn't exactly priority one. Horses get lost all the time."

Nancy wasn't about to be put off. "I think he was stolen."

"If you can prove it," McMillan said skeptically, "call me."

"I will," Nancy promised.

"In the meantime, be careful. In my book, that skyrocket wasn't an accident, or a prank." He glanced meaningfully at Tammy. "You have any enemies here?"

"No one who would want to hurt me," Tammy said.

Deputy McMillan glanced at his notes. "Some of the guests said a man from one of the banks in town had been here and insisted that you pay a bad loan."

Flushing, Tammy told him about her situation with Rob Majors and Vern Landon, and the officer scribbled more notes. A few minutes later, he turned his attention to the rest of the crowd. Another deputy searched the stables and house.

Tammy turned to the three friends. "I should never have involved you, Nancy," she said. "You're a guest at the ranch, and I want you to quit worrying about Renegade, Twister, and that—" She motioned helplessly to the still-smoldering car.

Nancy didn't agree. "I don't want to give up on this," she told Tammy. "Don't you see? We must be close to solving the case. The culprit is getting desperate."

"And dangerous." Tammy sighed. "Because of me, you and your friends were almost killed! This is supposed to be your vacation—not a deathtrap!"

"I know I'm close," Nancy insisted. "Whoever is behind Renegade's disappearance is starting to panic. I'm sure we can find him if we just have a little more time."

Tammy glanced at the deputies still poking around the burned car. "Okay," she finally said. "But if anything else happens, that's it!"

The next morning, Nancy examined the blackened car but found nothing the deputies had overlooked. She spent the rest of the day packing for the overnight campout planned for that night and searching the hills on the western edge of the Circle B on horseback. The area surrounding the Baineses' property—the westernmost portion of Misty Canyon—was particularly hilly, and General H lost his footing on the trail several times along the steep ridges.

But there was no sign of Renegade.

By late afternoon, Nancy returned to the ranch, only to saddle the pack horses and climb again onto General H's back. She and the rest of the campers rode single file up a steep trail to the campsite, a small clearing near a stream in the hills.

"I should've stayed back at the ranch," Bess complained as she untied her bedroll, then yanked the saddle from Marshmallow's back. "Every muscle in my body aches!"

George chuckled. "Think of all the fun we're

having, sleeping on rocks, cooking sourdough biscuits over an open fire, listening to the sounds of the night."

"Give me a break," Bess muttered.

Nancy placed her rolled sleeping bag on a bed of pine needles between the two cousins' bedrolls. Tucked in a private spot not too far from the campfire, their bags were sheltered by pine trees overhead.

While Mike, the Andersons, and a few men set up camp, Nancy, Bess, George, and the Hobarts searched for dried branches and twigs for the campfire.

Mrs. Mason flatly refused. With a sour look on her face, she plopped onto a tree stump. "I came here to relax, not to work," she stated, crossing her arms firmly over her chest.

"We all pitch in," Hank West told her as he tethered the horses.

"Some fun she's going to be," George remarked.

Bess swatted at a bee buzzing near her head. "Maybe she's got the right idea. Bees, mosquitoes, coyotes, and who knows what else seem to thrive around here."

"Probably cougars, bears, and wolves," George remarked.

"Thanks a lot," Bess replied. "Now I probably won't sleep a wink tonight!"

"Come on, it's going to be fun," Nancy told

them as she gathered an armload of branches. Though she would rather be investigating, she was determined to have a good time.

"Let me know when the fun starts," Bess suggested, but she smiled in spite of herself.

The entire group helped cook hash, biscuits, and coffee over the open fire. After dinner, they flipped a coin, and Sam and Ellen Anderson won the honors of doing dishes. Grumbling good-naturedly, Sam rolled up his sleeves.

"This will be good for him," Ellen said, winking at Nancy.

The rest of the group helped secure the horses and the camp.

Mike played guitar as shadows lengthened through the woods. Evening birds cooed, and the creek gurgled over stones. Through the branches overhead, Nancy could see the first stars winking in a lavender twilight sky.

Eventually, the dishes were finished and the camp secure. Mike put his guitar away. Hank poured everyone another cup of coffee and passed around a bag of Peggy's oatmeal cookies.

As night fell, the only light in the forest was the red glow from dying embers of the fire and a few pale beams filtering through the branches from the full moon.

"This isn't so bad after all," Bess admitted, adding three lumps of sugar to her coffee as she

110

sat cross-legged near the fire. "Maybe I will get some sleep after all."

A few minutes later, Bess and Nancy walked along a crooked trail to the creek to wash their faces. Nancy's flashlight beam bounced ahead, but she suddenly clicked the flashlight off and touched Bess's hand with hers. Bess understood the silent message and stopped short. Neither girl made a sound.

Nancy squinted through the trees and saw Mike Mathews talking softly with a young woman. Moonlight streamed through the branches, streaking the girl's pale hair with silver. The girl was Stella Baines! What was she doing with Mike? Stella wasn't part of the campout!

Signaling to Bess, Nancy moved forward slowly, her footsteps muffled by the pine needles. She strained to listen, but over the gurgle of the creek and the conversation back at the camp, she couldn't hear what Stella and Mike were saying.

". . . Twister . . . rodeo," Stella said.

". . . worry too much," Mike responded, patting her shoulder. Nancy leaned forward, holding her breath.

". . . go before I'm missed," he said, then turned and dashed through the trees.

Nancy followed Stella, hoping that the bareback rider would lead her to Renegade. Had Stella ridden him here?

Stella crossed the creek on a narrow log, climbed onto her bay mare, and took off toward the west end of the Circle B.

Nancy returned to the other side of the creek, where Bess was waiting. "Well?" Bess asked expectantly.

"I couldn't hear much. But Stella and Mike know more than they're telling. I heard them discussing the rodeo and Twister."

"I knew it!" Bess cried.

"Now, if only we can catch them," Nancy thought aloud. They started back toward the camp and ran into George.

"You must be squeaky clean by now," George observed. "Hank sent me looking for you."

"We'd better get back," Nancy said, then filled George in as they hurried along the trail.

"So what about Vern Landon and Rob Majors?" George asked. "Are they linked up with Mike and Stella?"

"I don't know," Nancy admitted, puzzled. "Either they're all in it together, or Landon's not involved at all."

"Maybe they're at cross purposes," George suggested. "They could be working against each other without even knowing it."

"You mean Stella and Mike are trying to keep Tammy out of the rodeo because Stella wants to win, and—"

George cut Bess off. "—Landon and Majors are

trying to force her to sell so they can get the ranch!"

"I wonder," Nancy said thoughtfully.

"Okay, folks," Hank said as the girls approached camp. He shot Nancy a questioning glance and said, "Let's call it a night. We have a long ride ahead of us tomorrow."

Nancy started for her sleeping bag but was surprised to see that the bag had been dragged several yards away from where she'd left it, farther in the trees. "That's odd," she said.

"What is?" Bess asked.

"My bag's been unrolled and moved."

"Well, move it back. Come on, I'm tired."

"Okay." Nancy reached for the bag but stopped when she heard an unfamiliar noise— like pebbles shaking together. Her skin crawled and her mouth went dry as she tugged on the bag. The noise stopped.

Nancy's heart was thudding. What was inside? Before she climbed into the bag, Nancy unzipped it carefully and tossed open the top flap.

Eyes glittered back at her in the dark. Nancy gasped. On the flannel lining was a coiled rattlesnake ready to strike!

11

Sidewinder!

Bess screamed, and George, reacting quickly, threw her own bag over the snake.

Mike sprinted across the campsite. "What's going on?"

"There's a rattlesnake in my bag!" Nancy said. Her gaze was glued to the writhing bags.

"A *what?*"

He pulled back George's bag, and the snake tried to escape by sidewinding toward the woods. But Mike was quick. He tossed the end of Nancy's sleeping bag over the snake again and, rolling it quickly, tied the bag with the cord. The snake was trapped inside, still wriggling as Mike dropped the bag onto the ground.

114

"How'd that happen?" Mike asked. His eyes narrowed.

"How'd *what* happen?" Hank asked, running from the makeshift corral where the horses were tethered.

"Nancy ended up with a rattlesnake in her bag."

Hank looked surprised. "Is this some kind of joke?" he demanded. "What do you think you're doing?"

"I had nothing to do with it! Someone unrolled my bag and put the snake in there," Nancy insisted. "I hadn't even unzipped my bedroll yet."

"That's impossi—"

"I'm not staying here another minute!" Mrs. Mason cut in. "I want to go back to the ranch!"

"Now, just simmer down," Hank suggested.

"Simmer down?" she repeated, astounded. *"Simmer down?* Not on your life! You're the ranch foreman—you find a way to get me off this mountain!"

Hank sighed loudly. "The way I see it, you've got two choices. Either you stay up here with the rest of the group, or you ride horseback in the dark through the trees with me for a couple hours until I find a safe spot and set this critter free."

Mrs. Mason gulped and glanced around the black, eerie woods. "I—I guess I'll stay," she decided, her voice trembling.

"Good." Hank snatched the wriggling bedroll from the ground. "Now, the rest of you, check your bags before you climb inside. Nancy, you can use my bedroll."

They all carefully opened their bags and shone flashlights in along the seams. All the sleeping bags were empty.

Nancy settled in between Bess and George. Closing her eyes, she tried to will herself to sleep, but her mind was churning with unanswered questions. Had Mike put the snake in her bag? Or Stella? But how—and when? In her mind's eye, she envisioned the frightened sidewinder trying to escape. A long time later, she finally dozed off.

The next morning was uneventful. The campers ate a breakfast of bacon and eggs, then broke camp.

On the ride back to the ranch, Bess groaned and shifted on Marshmallow's back. "All I want is a long, hot bubble bath, a couple of fashion magazines, and two hours in a soft bed."

"And all I want is to find Renegade," Nancy responded. She felt she was getting closer. She was sure Mike Mathews was the key.

Once they were back at the ranch and had cared for their horses, the girls returned to their rooms to clean up. Bess insisted on resting, but Nancy wanted to investigate Vern Landon. George agreed to drive into town with her for a visit to the library. They borrowed a pickup from Tammy, and, fortunately this time, they had no problem.

"I thought you had just about taken Vern Landon off the suspect list," George remarked as they parked in front of a cement-block building on the main street of the small town.

"I just want to make sure," Nancy said. She pocketed the keys. "I really think Mike's involved somehow, but I don't want to leave any stone unturned."

In the air-conditioned library, Nancy and George searched through old newspapers and microfiche, learning as much as they could about Vern Landon. There were several articles on him and the land he had developed in Montana, but his reputation seemed clean and reputable.

"Looks like a dead end," George said, rubbing her eyes.

"Maybe," Nancy agreed. "Besides, he would have had to have an accomplice working with him, someone at the ranch who could do his dirty work with Renegade, the car, and the snake."

"Someone like Mike Mathews?"

Nancy nodded. "But I've never seen them together. It just doesn't fit." Placing the final case of microfiche back into the drawer of the metal file cabinet, she sighed, her thoughts still jumbled. "I guess that leaves us with Stella and Mike."

"You think they're in it together?"

"They must be," Nancy said as she walked down one aisle, but she stopped when she spied a long row of encyclopedias. "Wait a minute," she said, pulling out the S volume.

"Now what?"

"Remember the snake last night?" Nancy thumbed through the pages.

"How could I forget?"

"Something about it bothered me."

"A *lot* of things about it bothered *me*," George remarked. She leaned over Nancy's shoulder.

Nancy found the section on rattlesnakes and studied the pictures. "They're all different— diamondbacks, timber snakes, sidewinders. There are even eastern and western versions."

"Our 'friend' comes from a big family. So what?"

Nancy's blue eyes twinkled. She snapped the volume shut. "I know what it is!" she exclaimed.

"So tell!"

"That snake wasn't from this area, George! Remember how it crawled sideways? It was a desert sidewinder!" Nancy met her friend's eyes. "There's no desert in Misty Canyon."

George's brows shot up. "A clue. But what does it mean?"

"I'm not sure," Nancy conceded. "But I intend to find out!" As they walked out of the cool library and climbed into the truck, Nancy went on, "It doesn't quite fit. Mike seems to care about the horses. I don't think he'd intentionally risk hurting Twister or Renegade."

As they approached the turnoff for Calloway Dude Ranch, Nancy stepped on the accelerator, driving past the lane.

"Hey, where are you going?" George asked.

"I think it's time we had a talk with Stella Baines," Nancy replied with a smile.

"I doubt if she'll want to."

"Let's just see what she has to say."

The Circle B was as different from Calloway Dude Ranch as night from day. All the buildings were freshly stained a deep redwood color, and the main house sparkled white in the late-afternoon sun. With a broad front porch, columns, and green shutters on the windows, the three-story house looked like it belonged on a southern plantation.

"Look at this place," George said with a soft whistle.

Ranch hands and guests were scattered in the tree-shaded yard, and the bustle of activity filled the air. Children laughed as they played on a wooden playground or rode ponies. The tantalizing smell of roasting chicken caused Nancy's stomach to growl, reminding her that she had missed lunch.

"This looks more like an anthill than a dude ranch," George observed as they climbed out of the pickup. "It's swarming with workers!" Stable boys walked horses and instructed the guests on care of the horses. Ranch hands came and went, doing chores.

Nancy knocked on the front door and was greeted by a severe-looking, graying blond woman in her fifties. With thin lips, she introduced herself as Joy Baines, Nathaniel's sister.

"What can I do for you?" she asked, blocking the doorway.

"We're looking for Stella," Nancy said.

"Are you fans of hers?" the woman asked.

"Actually, we're guests at the Calloway Dude Ranch. Tammy asked us to help her find Renegade."

"I heard he escaped," Joy Baines said, the edges of her full lips turning down. "It was bound to happen, you know. That stallion has a mean streak that won't quit. But Stella wouldn't know anything about the horse." The woman glanced at her watch. "She should be back any minute."

"Back?" Nancy asked. "Where is she?"

Joy Baines eyed her warily. "She's practicing, and she prefers to do it in private, away from all the hubbub of the ranch." Grudgingly, she added, "You can wait inside if you like."

"Is it possible to talk with Stella's father?"

Joy Baines frowned. "I don't know. Nathaniel

went into town earlier, but he should be back. Why don't you check with one of the hands?"

"Thanks," Nancy said as the woman shoved the door closed in her face.

They asked a young stable boy who was repairing a fence about Nathaniel, and he pointed to a long, low building he referred to as the zoo.

"The zoo?" George repeated.

"That's right. The reptile zoo," the hand said. "Haven't you heard of it? You'd better wait outside, though. Mr. Baines doesn't want anyone in there today."

Nancy and George exchanged glances. "Why not?" Nancy asked.

The hand shrugged. "I don't know. The foreman just said it was off-limits. If I see Mr. Baines, I'll tell him you're waiting up at the house."

"Sure," Nancy said. She and George headed back to the main house. When the ranch hand turned his attention to his work, Nancy ducked behind one of the outbuildings, pulling George with her. They walked between two fences to the back door of the zoo.

"You don't suppose they happen to have an exhibit of desert sidewinders in here, do you?" Nancy asked George.

"Let's find out."

Together they pushed open the door and walked past the glass cages of exotic animals.

There were snakes, horned toads, lizards, turtles, and a few desert rodents. Nancy made her way through the cages but stopped short when she heard an angry hissing behind her. She turned to find a small Gila monster glaring at her.

"Look, Nancy, over here!" George pointed to an empty glass cage. The nameplate made it clear that a desert sidewinder was the missing inhabitant.

The door opened with a bang. "Get away from there!" Nathaniel Baines shouted, his face red with fury. "No one's supposed to be in here! There's a rattler loose!"

"I know," Nancy replied. "I found him in my sleeping bag last night."

Nathaniel stopped dead in his tracks. At that moment, Nancy noticed his belt and its flashing silver buckle, just like the one she'd seen as she'd been attacked in Twister's stall. "You found it *where*?" Nathaniel bellowed.

Nancy explained about the campout and the sidewinder but left out the part about seeing his daughter with Mike Mathews.

At first unconvinced, Nathaniel listened and shook his head. "You're sure about this?" he asked, lifting his hat and wiping sweat from his forehead with a handkerchief. "Hank West let my snake go?"

"He didn't know it was yours," Nancy pointed out.

Nathaniel's neck turned dark red. "So how did the sidewinder get up at the campsite in your bag?"

"Someone put it there—someone who can handle snakes."

He glanced nervously away from Nancy's eyes. "That could be anyone on this ranch," Nathaniel said. "But I trust my hands implicitly—ever since Mathews left, we haven't had any trouble."

"You mean Mike Mathews?"

Nathaniel's jaw hardened. "He's a criminal, that one. I wouldn't put a stunt like this past him—he'd probably do it just to get back at me."

"So all your hands can work with snakes?" George asked.

"Absolutely. And they know how to treat snakebite, too. Those rattlers are dangerous!"

"Has Mike Mathews been around lately?" Nancy asked.

"Not on your life!" Nathaniel scowled darkly. "I won't allow him to set foot on this place. He used to see my daughter, Stella, but I put a stop to that when I caught him thieving."

"Stella doesn't date him anymore?" Nancy asked.

"Of course not! She realizes that he was just a cheap hand trying to get in good with her because of this ranch and all the money it's worth. She doesn't have time for people like Mathews. She's too busy with that rodeo coming up on the fourth. If Stella wins that prize, she'll get a commercial endorsement and maybe a part in a movie, plus a national rodeo tour!"

"So it's important to her," Nancy murmured.

"Very. It could change her life," Nathaniel said proudly as he ushered the girls outside. He glanced at the sun hanging over the hills on the west end of the spread. "I guess I'd better drive over to the Calloway place right now and find out how Hank intends paying me for my snake." Still muttering under his breath, he stalked through the door.

Nancy and George found their way back to the pickup.

"So it looks like Mike's our man," George said.

"Maybe." Nancy started the pickup and drove down the gravel lane. "How about a soda?" she asked, and George nodded eagerly. They drove to the Williams store, and each bought a bottle of cola.

As they drove back to Calloway Ranch, Nancy said, "If Mike really cares about Stella, why would he want her to win the rodeo? That would mean she might move away."

"Yeah, but he's a bronco rider himself, right? He could follow her. And that would get her away from her dad. Or maybe he's just doing it because it's what *she* wants." George glanced fondly at her friend. "You've been known to go out of your way to help a certain football quarter-back at Emerson College."

Nancy smiled at the thought of Ned Nickerson, her longtime boyfriend. She missed Ned right now and wished he were there. Sometimes just talking to Ned made the most complex cases easier to deal with.

Nancy and George met Nathaniel Baines as he was driving out of Calloway Ranch and they were driving in. He didn't even wave as he passed. His eyes were glued to the road ahead, and his expression was dark.

"I wonder what happened?" George asked.

"I guess we'll have to wait to find out." Nancy parked the pickup just as the dinner bell rang loudly.

"That's my cue," George said. "I'm starved!"

"Me too!"

Together they walked toward the main house, but as they climbed the steps, Bess burst through the screen door. Her face was white, and she swallowed hard.

"Thank goodness you're back," Bess cried. "It—it's Renegade! Something terrible has happened!"

12

Bullwhip

"Renegade?" Nancy asked. "Where is he?"

"Tammy found a note slipped under the kitchen door, and it's just awful!" Bess said, biting her lower lip.

"Where is she?"

"Up in her room."

Nancy didn't waste any time. Rushing past Bess, Nancy dashed into the house, bounded up the stairs two at a time, and tore into Tammy's room. George and Bess followed. They found Tammy sitting on the windowsill, staring across the fields. Her shoulders were slumped, and she held a piece of white paper in her hands.

Tammy glanced at the three friends, her eyes

meeting Nancy's. "You were right," she said as Nancy crossed the room to her. "Someone has stolen Renegade!" Angrily, she crumpled the note in her fist. "Who would do this to me?"

"I have a few ideas about that," Nancy said.

Tammy handed the wadded piece of paper to her, and Nancy skimmed the short typewritten message: "T.C.—If you enter the Independence Day Rodeo, Renegade dies! I've already stolen your horse and set off the fireworks in your car. I mean business!"

Nancy made a quick decision. "Tammy, tell me all you know about Mike Mathews."

Tammy's green eyes widened. "Mike isn't involved in this."

"You don't know that," Nancy said. "Whoever stole Renegade had to be someone who knows this ranch inside and out, and someone who has access to your car."

"That could be lots of people."

"Can lots of people handle live rattlesnakes and know something about fireworks? That snake was a desert sidewinder, not a timber rattler. It was taken from the Circle B. Nathaniel Baines thinks Mike stole the snake out of revenge."

Tammy clenched her teeth. "Nathaniel was just here demanding payment for his snake! When Hank found out the rattler was from the Circle B, he really told Nathaniel off! Hank's never much liked Nathaniel," she said more calmly. "He seems to think that the Circle B is responsible for things going bad around here."

"And you don't?" Nancy prodded.

"We've just had a string of bad luck ever since Renegade threw Dad."

Nancy wondered. She read the threatening letter again. "Did all your bad luck start when you hired Mike Mathews?"

"Oh, no. Mike's been great!"

"He does have a criminal past," Bess reminded Tammy. "He stole from guests at the Circle B."

"But I can't believe he would hurt Renegade." Tammy squared her shoulders defensively. "He's been a big help around this place, and he's trying to change."

"He did say some pretty nasty things about that horse," George pointed out.

"That's because he blames Renegade for Dad's death, even though it's not true. He and Hank both think that the fall Dad took while trying to ride Renegade robbed Dad of his will to live." Tammy stood and took the note from Nancy's outstretched hand. "Even though he's not crazy about Renegade, Mike really does love animals. Especially horses. You know, I'd almost believe that he would booby-trap the car before hurting any of the livestock." Frowning, she studied the short message. "Why would Mike want to hurt me?"

"Maybe he doesn't," Nancy suggested. "Maybe he just wants to help Stella. That reference about the rodeo must be because of Stella. If you don't enter, she has a much better shot at winning the bareback competition."

Tammy shook her head. "I don't know what to think."

"Just don't withdraw from the rodeo in Boise. At least not yet," Nancy suggested. "Now, tell me. Do you have any typewriters on the ranch?"

"Just one, in the den. But this note wasn't written on it. The letters are different."

"I think you'd better show this note to Deputy McMillan," Nancy suggested. "Maybe then he'll take Renegade's disappearance more seriously."

The dinner bell rang again. "Come on," George urged. "I'm starved!"

"I'm not hungry," Tammy said. "I'll be down in a little while. Please tell Peggy not to worry."

"That's like telling a rooster not to crow," George whispered to Nancy once they were in the corridor. "That woman is a born worrier."

"Wait until she hears about her nephew," Bess added. "It'll break her heart. She got Mike this job, you know."

"It's a mess any way you look at it," Nancy admitted. She hurried to her room to comb her hair. She couldn't dislodge the feeling that she'd overlooked something. Tonight, after dinner, she'd go over every clue and see what she could come up with. If she found nothing to change her mind, she'd have to confront Mike Mathews with the truth.

After dinner, everyone seemed content and settled, but Nancy was restless. She stared through the windows to the steep hills surrounding Misty Canyon. Somewhere—and Mike Mathews probably knew just where—Renegade was hidden.

Maybe there was a clue in the bunkhouse or something she had overlooked in the tack room. This was her opportunity to find out. After whispering her plans to George, she slipped upstairs, tucked her hair into a Stetson, and grabbed her jeans jacket and flashlight. Then, hardly making a sound, she took the back stairs through the kitchen and hurried outside.

Clouds were gathering in the sky, and a cool wind brushed her cheeks as she walked briskly along a path leading to the bunkhouse. She knocked on the bunkhouse door. No one answered.

Holding her breath, she pushed the door open.

The bunkhouse had one large sleeping room, a bathroom, and several lockers. She swept the beam of her flashlight over the names on the lockers and located a banged-up door with Mike Mathews's name taped above the lock. Nancy tried the handle. Creaking loudly, the door swung open.

As quickly as possible, Nancy searched through Mike's things. She found nothing except the belt with the silver buckle that was just like the one she'd seen before she was knocked out. Although she glanced through a small pile of papers at the bottom of the locker and even checked inside his boots, she found nothing to link him to Renegade's disappearance.

After closing the locker, Nancy quietly stole out of the bunkhouse. She glanced at the main house and around the yard. No one seemed to have missed her. Through the windows, she could see the guests still gathered in the living room. Deciding it was now or never, she ducked behind a hedge leading to the tack room.

The windowless tack room smelled of oiled leather. She shone her beam on the hanging gear. Bridles jangled as she inadvertently brushed against the hanging reins, but nothing looked out of place. Nancy searched through Mike's riding gear and saddle bags but came up empty.

Frustrated, she glanced at her watch. She'd been gone nearly half an hour. If she didn't return to the main house soon, someone might come looking for her.

She opened the medicine cabinet as an afterthought. In the pale beam of her flashlight, she read the label of each tube and bottle, hoping to find something that would explain Twister's odd behavior. But the ointments and creams didn't seem out of the ordinary.

There's got to be something, she told herself. Reaching around a bottle of peroxide, she found a jar of medication she hadn't noticed before. She pulled it out and was reading the label when she heard the sound of a boot scrape behind her.

She nearly dropped the jar as she jammed it into her pocket. She switched off her flashlight. She crouched low against the wall, hoping to hide in the shadows. She hardly dared to breathe. Was the sound inside the tack room? Or in the yard outside?

With her heart hammering double-time, she turned slowly, looking over her shoulder to see the silhouette of a tall, broad-shouldered man in the doorway. He raised his arm.

To her horror, Nancy saw a bullwhip in his hand. He moved as if knowing instinctively where she hid. She shrank back. The man flicked his wrist. Like a pistol shot, the whip cracked, sizzling through the air at her face!

13

Another Escape

Nancy jumped aside as the whip sliced only inches from where she'd been. She snapped on her flashlight and shone the beam right into Mike Mathews's baffled face.

"Who is it?" he asked, reaching for the switch on the wall and throwing on the lights.

Nancy shook her hair out of her hat.

"Nancy?" He seemed genuinely surprised. "What're you doing snooping around here?"

"Trying to prove that Twister hasn't gone bad."

He frowned. "Oh, that again. Sometimes I forget you're such a *great* detective."

Nancy ignored the insult. "And what are you doing with that?" She pointed at the whip.

Some of his anger melted. "I guess I owe you an apology. I thought you were the thief who took the Masons' things. I saw someone sneak in here, and I thought I'd give him a scare. I didn't realize it was you. Sorry." He shrugged. "But if I'd wanted to hit you, I could have." To prove his point, he snapped off the lights for a minute, raised the whip, and flicked his wrist. The whip cracked again, and this time the tip hit the medicine cabinet door, and it swung shut.

Mike turned on the lights and crossed his arms over his chest. "I didn't mean to scare you, but you really shouldn't be here. All these crazy notions you've got about the horses don't hold any water, you know."

"No?" Nancy asked, walking closer and holding his gaze. "Then how do you explain Renegade's disappearance?"

"He took off. Period."

"You had nothing to do with it?"

Mike's expression hardened. "So you still don't believe me." He snorted in frustration. "You think this jailbird had something to do with the horses acting strangely and escaping. Well, you're barking up the wrong tree. Believe it or not, I work here just like anyone else. Why would I want to steal Renegade or drug Twister?"

"To spoil Tammy's chances in the rodeo."

"To what?" He grinned crookedly, and Nancy

134

had the distinct impression that he was laughing at her. "I don't follow you. I want Tammy to win." He started for the door.

Nancy took a gamble and asked, "Even if it means Stella will lose?"

Mike whirled. His eyes glinted like steel, and his fist coiled tightly over the handle of his whip. "You actually think I would sabotage Tammy's chances of winning?"

"Wouldn't you? For Stella?"

"Look, I've made more than my share of mistakes in the past. But I'm not about to make any more. Sure, I care for Stella, but she's got to make it on her own—stand up against the competition." He jerked a thumb at his chest. "I'm a rodeo rider myself, and I believe that if you're the best, you have to prove it. Stella *has* to face Tammy, to prove herself."

"Is that how Stella feels?"

He glanced away. "I can't speak for her."

Nancy crossed the room and stood in the doorway. "How important *is* the Independence Day Rodeo to Stella?"

He swallowed. "Very."

"Why?"

"That's none of your business."

"It is. Tammy received a death threat against Renegade unless she drops out of the rodeo."

Mike answered quickly, too quickly. "Maybe it

was from that jerk that's giving her a rough time at the bank. What's his name—Majors? He and Vern Landon are both hounding her."

Nancy shook her head. "They couldn't have put a snake in my sleeping bag. I doubt if either man knows how to handle rattlers, and they weren't anywhere near the campfire. I checked. Also, they didn't have time to put the fireworks under the car."

"But Stella couldn't have—" His shoulders slumped. "You think I did that? That I would try to kill you?"

"Or Tammy," Nancy said.

"That's ridiculous!"

"Just tell me why this rodeo is so important to Stella Baines," Nancy demanded.

Mike's nostrils flared. "So she can get out from under her dad's thumb, all right? So she can win and get a huge commercial endorsement, maybe even get a part in a movie. This rodeo is worth big bucks! Is that so hard to understand?"

Nancy thought about the close relationship she had with her own father. "Maybe Stella should talk things out with her dad."

"Believe me, it's beyond that point," Mike insisted. "Old man Baines wants to control her and manage her career, even tell her who she can and can't see."

"Including you?"

"*Especially* me."

Nancy pushed. "I bet she would do anything to get away from him."

"Not anything, Nancy. Stella wouldn't do anything so crazy and dangerous as the stunts that have been happening around here. And if you don't believe me, you can ask her yourself. I left her not ten minutes ago."

Nancy was surprised and worried. Any time Stella was on the Calloway Ranch, there was bound to be trouble. "Where?"

"By the lake," he replied hotly. "Stella has to sneak over here to see me because her dad disapproves." As if realizing he'd said too much, he pushed past her and strode angrily across the yard, his boots crunching on the wet gravel.

Nancy shut off the light, then noticed the dark clouds filling the sky. She turned the collar of her jacket against the first cool breath of wind and dashed across the yard to the lake. She searched the dock area but couldn't find any trace of Stella.

Unnerved, Nancy hurried up the back stairs of the main house. She found Tammy in her room, sitting back against the pillows on her bed.

Nancy dug in her pocket and extracted the small bottle of medicine. It was half full. "What's this?" she asked. "Could it have been used on Twister?"

Tammy read the label and shook her head. "If it was, he'd fall asleep. This is a depressant, Nancy. We use it rarely. Once in a while, a horse is injured and goes into a frenzy. We give this to calm it down."

Nancy sighed in frustration as Bess walked into the room. "I wondered where you were, Nancy. George and I were beginning to get worried." She polished a bright red apple against her checked blouse, then took a bite.

Nancy watched her friend, then smiled, her blue eyes dancing. "That's it!" she cried as the puzzle began to unravel in her mind. "Bess, you're a genius!"

"I am?" Bess was baffled.

"The apple! That's how the drug was given to Renegade! I saw a half-eaten apple in his stall the night he disappeared, but the next time I looked the apple was gone!"

"Hey, whoa! Slow down," Bess insisted as George joined the group in Tammy's room. "I thought you thought that *Twister* had been drugged! Renegade's disappeared, remember?"

Excited, Nancy exclaimed, "But I was wrong. The horses were switched! *Renegade* didn't escape that night. It was Twister. Someone deliberately let him out—or rode him. That's why I thought I saw a rider on his back. No one can ride Renegade, but Twister's known for his sweet disposition. I think *Renegade*'s been drugged with this depressant!" She held up the jar.

Tammy's eyes widened. "That would mean

that I was really riding Renegade the day I was thrown!"

"Yes! And it would explain why Twister has supposedly gone bad!" George added.

Nancy nodded. "I think Stella Baines deliberately switched the horses to keep you out of the Independence Day Rodeo."

"Stella?" Tammy gasped. "I can't believe it."

"She has motive *and* opportunity. I saw her with Mike on the night of the campout. She must have brought the rattlesnake and put it in my bag. And she was here the day the Masons' things were stolen."

"And she was at the barbecue," Bess said.

"She was here earlier today to meet Mike. Maybe she slipped the note about Renegade under the kitchen door!" George said.

"But she wouldn't set off an explosion," Tammy protested.

Nancy was convinced. "Either she did or Mike helped her."

"So you still suspect him," Tammy said.

"He claims he's innocent. But I'm not sure he can be trusted."

"Hey, wait a minute!" George cut in. "There's one major hole in your theory, Nancy. If Twister and Renegade were really switched, why didn't we notice the difference? Isn't Twister supposed to have some sort of white mark on his leg?"

"Simple," Nancy replied, grinning. "Peroxide. Stella drugged Renegade, then bleached the hairs on his fetlock in the crescent pattern. That's why some of the straw in Renegade's stall was whiter than the rest. The peroxide had spilled."

"So Stella or Mike switched halters, then put Renegade in Twister's stall," George said, following Nancy's train of thought.

"And that's why Twister was acting up! Twister was really Renegade!" Nancy pointed out, unraveling the mystery for everyone in the room.

Tammy pushed her pen and papers aside. "Well, let's see if you're right. I should be able to tell if the white mark on Twister's leg is real or not."

"And then we'll talk with Stella," Nancy said. "My guess is that she's still here somewhere." Nancy didn't add that she'd already checked the dock. She was uneasy about Stella being on the ranch, but she didn't want to upset Tammy any more than necessary.

"If I find out that she's done anything to Twister, Stella will have to answer to me personally!" Tammy vowed. Her green eyes snapped as she took the back stairs and dashed through the kitchen.

Nancy, Bess, and George followed. Outside, the wind had picked up, and rain peppered the gravel. A streak of lightning flashed over the surrounding hills.

140

Tammy yanked open the door of the stallion barn and switched on the light. Gasping, she stopped short.

Twister's stall was empty!

A cold feeling settled in the pit of Nancy's stomach.

"What now?" George asked.

Nancy ran through the barn to the far end of the stalls. The back door was open. It caught against the wind and banged against the outside wall. Rain blew inside, puddling on the concrete floor. Renegade was gone!

14

Renegade Ride

"He's gone, isn't he?" Tammy asked, sick at heart.

"Not for long," Nancy declared. She closed the door of the barn and turned to find Mike Mathews striding into the building from the main entrance. "Stella's stolen Renegade *and* Twister," Nancy told him.

He glanced at Twister's empty stall. "What do you mean?"

Tammy said, "Nancy thinks the horses were switched, that Stella rode Twister out of here a few nights ago, and that the horse she left in Twister's stall was really Renegade."

"That's impossible—those two horses act so different!"

Tammy explained Nancy's theory and looked Mike steadily in the eye. "Nancy also thinks you might have had something to do with everything that's gone on around here."

"I already told her I didn't," Mike snapped. But he added quickly, "And I don't think Stella had any part in this."

"Then prove it," Nancy suggested, her mind spinning ahead to the only logical place Stella could have hidden Twister. "Help me find the horses."

Mike didn't back down. "I'd be glad to."

"Good. Tell me about Stella's private corral— the place where she practices. Where is it?"

Mike studied the determined set of Nancy's jaw and hesitated. "Stella doesn't like company. And I already asked her if she'd seen the horse."

"So where does she practice?"

Mike wrestled with his conscience a minute, then said, "At the west end of Misty Canyon. There's a sort of a natural box in the cliffs."

"Hank's men searched that area," Tammy said to Nancy. "And they talked with Stella."

But Nancy wasn't deterred. "Is there any shelter for her horses up there? A barn?"

"Just a lean-to she uses for hay," Mike said. "But, yes, it's big enough for a horse or two."

George said, "Stella could've hidden Twister inside, and Hank's men wouldn't have noticed."

"Now, wait a minute—" Mike protested.

Nancy asked, "How do I get there?"

"You don't," Mike said, taking a stand. "There are no roads, and it's a stormy night. You'd never find the place."

"He's right," Tammy said. "I know those hills, and it would be impossible to try to follow the trail. It runs along the stream and winds through the foothills."

"The stream where I lost Twister before?" Nancy asked.

"Right. It's a couple of miles up the creek from that point," Tammy said.

"That's all I need to know," Nancy said, then turned to George. "Call the sheriff's office and talk to Deputy McMillan. Tell him what I'm doing, and ask him to send officers here and to the Circle B."

"What are you planning to do?" Mike demanded.

Nancy smiled. "I'm either going to expose Stella for the horse thief she is or end up looking like a bad detective." She turned and ran to the trail horse barn.

Tammy was right behind her, matching her strides. "This is too dangerous, Nancy!" she exclaimed, waving toward the hills. "Look at that storm. Please wait!"

Lightning cracked across the sky. "It might be too late already," Nancy replied as she hoisted a saddle onto General H's back and tightened the cinch. "Stella knows I'm on to her. There's no time to lose. She probably had to lead Renegade out of here because she couldn't ride him, even if he was drugged. That should slow her down a little. Let's just hope I can find her before she does anything stupid."

"You don't really think she'd hurt Renegade, do you?"

"I hope not," Nancy said. She led General H outside, swung into the saddle, and pressed her heels into the buckskin's ribs.

As General H leapt forward, Nancy snapped on her flashlight and squinted through the driving rain. She knew that George and Bess would contact the sheriff.

If only she wasn't too late!

General H galloped across the rain-slickened fields and into the woods. Though the forest was dark and gloomy, Nancy let her horse find his way along the path through the pines.

Wind whistled through the branches overhead, and twice General H shied. At last, the woods gave way to a clearing and the ridge where Renegade—or Twister, as Nancy suspected— had disappeared several nights before.

The buckskin balked at the edge of the ravine, but Nancy urged him forward. Stumbling, he slid down the steep embankment to the crooked stream. Nancy turned west and followed the trail along the bank, her heart pounding in excitement when she noticed fresh tracks along the wet banks. She was right! Stella had obviously ridden through here!

Lightning sizzled through the hills in the distance, and thunder rumbled across the sky. Rain slid down her neck. Nancy was cold to the bone by the time the trail led away from the creek and through a thicket of trees.

Then General H's ears pricked up, and Nancy stopped. Straining, she heard the sound of an engine starting before fading away. Stella must have parked her truck here, then ridden her horse to Calloway Ranch to steal the stallion, Nancy reasoned. Now Stella had driven off.

Good, Nancy thought. She could rescue Tammy's two stallions without a confrontation. When Stella returned to the Circle B, she would have to face Deputy McMillan.

Clucking her tongue, Nancy kicked the General softly. Her horse rounded a final bend, and the trees gave way to open land surrounded on three sides by steep cliffs.

"So this is it," she whispered, squinting against the rain. She noticed the rails and gate that blocked off the end of the canyon. Within the enclosure, she saw a racing track, some oil drums used in barrel racing, and a lean-to that was little more than a shack. Renegade and Twister had to be inside!

General H fidgeted and snorted as Nancy tied the reins of his bridle over the top rail. She vaulted the fence, then sloshed her way through the mud to the shack.

Horses nickered from within the small lean-to. Shoving hard on the door, Nancy forced her way into the musty-smelling single room. Rain dripped against the roof and ran inside down the cracks in the walls.

Nancy moved her flashlight across the dark interior. A stallion shrieked as Nancy shone her flashlight inside, and Nancy grinned as she recognized Renegade—or was it Twister? It didn't matter. The black stallions, both blindfolded, and Stella's horse were tied to the far end of the room.

Nancy untied Twister and Renegade and led them, kicking and pulling, through the small door. "Come on," she said, trying to quiet them both, but they tossed their heads wildly, rearing and nearly pulling Nancy's arms out of their sockets. Her boots slid in the mud, and the reins cut into her palms. If the two horses hadn't been blindfolded, she wouldn't have been able to control them.

Lightning streaked across the sky as Nancy opened the gate. Rain pounded the earth, and, from far in the distance, she heard the sound of an engine whining. Was it the sheriff's department or Stella? She stopped and listened. Her heart sank as she realized the noise was getting closer.

Twin beams of headlights cut through the rain just as thunder rumbled overhead. Then a horn blasted, echoing through the canyon.

General H spooked, rearing backward and yanking so hard on the reins that the top rail of the fence snapped, setting him free. He tore off, hooves thundering.

Nancy was stranded!

She had no choice but to ride one of the rodeo stallions. They both reared wildly. Which was Renegade and which was Twister?

Nancy didn't have time to find out.

She pulled them closer to the fence, climbed on the top rail, yanked off their blindfolds, and jumped onto the back of one stallion. With the fingers of her right hand around his lead rope and entwined in his mane, she gave him a quick kick. She held tightly to the lead rope of the other horse with her free hand.

Nancy's mount leapt forward. Across the flat, muddy ground they tore. The pickup, horn blasting, wheels spinning, roared after them. Rain beat down from the cloud-covered sky. Nancy could barely see. The powerful horse beneath her ran crazily toward the woods, his sleek muscles bunching and extending.

"Come on, come on," Nancy said, nearly losing

her balance as he leapt into the air and shied at the sound of the horn. Nancy looked over her shoulder as lightning flashed again. She could clearly see Stella in the driver's seat, and the pickup was closing the gap!

She leaned forward just as her mount ducked into the scrub trees and ran along the banks of the creek. Water splashed from his powerful legs, and twice he stumbled.

Nancy prayed that the truck couldn't follow, but the engine didn't falter. Stella drove her rig through the trees, then down the middle of the stream after them, honking her horn wildly. She was so close now that Nancy was sure the terrified horse behind would fall and be crushed by the truck!

Suddenly, a horrifying explosion sounded. Stella was shooting at her!

A sizzling object whizzed over Nancy's head. Fireworks! Stella was setting off skyrockets, hoping to spook the horses!

The first rocket exploded to the left, sending a spray of blinding green light throughout the rain-drizzled forest. The stallion reared and screamed. Nancy pitched forward but managed to stay astride.

The next skyrocket burst a few feet in front of the horse, and he shuddered before lunging high into the air.

Nancy hung on for dear life. "Hold on, boy,"

she said, urging him up the surrounding hills. She couldn't reach for her flashlight unless she let go of the horse behind her, but she wasn't about to lose Tammy's stallions. Not now!

Another skyrocket sprayed sparks behind them, and the back horse bolted, nearly ripping Nancy off her mount. Nancy's arms ached, but she wouldn't let go! Her stallion scrambled up a bank. Nancy expected a skyrocket to land at any minute, but the whistling and explosions stopped abruptly. Stella must have given up.

Gasping, Nancy clung to her horse as he tore up an embankment.

Suddenly, light flooded the area. For a minute, she thought Stella had circled around and was using the pickup's headlights to blind her. She was about to shout for help when she realized that she wasn't looking into headlights at all. Before her was a group of riders with a searchlight—a group of riders she couldn't have been happier to see!

George was on Whirlwind, Tammy on a big roan, Hank and Mike on their horses, and even Bess was there, astride Marshmallow. They were all very wet but relieved to see Nancy.

Nancy wanted to shout for joy.

She slid to the ground and gave her mount's reins to Hank.

"We called Deputy McMillan," George said.

"He went straight over to the Circle B to arrest Stella for horse thieving."

Nancy looked through the rain to Mike Mathews, who said, "I guess I owe you another apology, Nancy."

In the distance, through the pounding rain, Nancy heard the scream of sirens and knew that Stella would finally be captured.

"I owe you a big favor," Tammy said, dismounting. "And I want you and your friends to stay an extra week at the ranch—free of charge!"

"I hope that doesn't mean we have more kitchen duty," George said with a laugh.

"No way," Tammy replied. Then she stared at the horse Nancy had ridden. She examined his fetlock and gasped. "This is Renegade," she whispered in awe. "You actually rode him!"

"How about that?" Hank murmured.

Nancy smiled weakly at the thought. "He was drugged . . . remember?"

"Come on," Tammy suggested. "You can double up with me. We need to get you back to the ranch to dry out."

The next day, Deputy McMillan stopped by Calloway Ranch. The sun had broken through the clouds, and though the ground was still damp, the air was fresh and clean. Nancy, Bess, George, and Tammy were sitting on the front porch, drinking lemonade and eating apple fritters, as he approached.

He strode up the steps and took off his sunglasses. "I thought you'd want to know that Stella confessed to everything," he told Tammy. "Mike Mathews wasn't involved at all."

"I already knew that," Tammy said. "I believed what he told me."

"Stella switched the horses and rode Twister out of here, just as Miss Drew figured. She even admitted to rigging the car with the fireworks and planting the snake in the sleeping bag," McMillan reported. "Every day she'd manage to drive over here on the pretense of seeing Mike, then drug the horse. You almost caught her at it, Nancy, and she had to knock you out."

"What about the Masons' wallet and purse?" Bess asked.

"She did that when you were all outside, and she typed the threatening note on her father's typewriter. She's confessed to it all."

"Were Vern Landon and Rob Majors involved?"

McMillan sighed and took the glass of lemonade Nancy had poured for him. "The way I hear it, the bank Majors works for is not at all happy about the way he handled everything. He's made some enemies, and the bank's embarrassed. As for Landon, he'll probably just move on to the next land deal." He took a long swallow from his glass, then turned to Tammy. "Are you going to press charges against Stella Baines?"

"I'll think about it," Tammy said. "Maybe it would be better if she had to ride against me in the rodeo."

The deputy smiled. "Are you that sure of winning?"

Tammy tossed her hair out of her eyes confidently. "Sooner or later, Stella and I will have to compete. Now that I've got Twister back, I think I've got a good chance, thanks to Nancy Drew."

"That reminds me," McMillan said. "Miss Drew, you rode Renegade last night! I thought he was billed as the horse no man could ride."

"He was," Nancy replied with a dimpled smile. "But he wasn't billed as the horse no *woman* could ride!"